GUNNER

AN EIDOLON BLACK OPS NOVEL: BOOK 6

MADDIE WADE

Gunner
An Eidolon Black Ops Novel: Book 6
by Maddie Wade

Published by Maddie Wade
Copyright © February 2021 Maddie Wade

Cover: Envy Creative Designs
Editing: Black Opal Editing
Formatting: Black Opal Editing

CONTENTS

Acknowledgments 1
Author's Note 2
Prologue 4
Chapter 1 9
Chapter 2 13
Chapter 3 18
Chapter 4 23
Chapter 5 31
Chapter 6 37
Chapter 7 44
Chapter 8 50
Chapter 9 55
Chapter 10 62
Chapter 11 68
Chapter 12 74
Chapter 13 79
Chapter 14 84
Chapter 15 90
Chapter 16 95
Chapter 17 100
Chapter 18 104
Chapter 19 110
Chapter 20 117
Chapter 21 124
Chapter 22 129
Chapter 23 134
Chapter 24 139
Chapter 25 145
Chapter 26 150
Chapter 27 154
Epilogue 159
Sneak Peek: Waggs 162
Books by Maddie Wade 168
About the Author 171

Acknowledgments

I am so lucky to have such an amazing team around me, without which I could never bring these books to life. I am so grateful to have you in my life. You are more than friends you are so essential to my life.

My wonderful beta team, Greta and Deanna who are brutally honest and beautifully kind. If it is rubbish you tell me it is, and if you love it you are effusive. Your support means so much to me.

To the ladies of Words Whiskey and Wine for Woman, you are my crew and I love you.

My editor—Linda at Black Opal Editing, who is so patient. She is so much more than an editor she is a teacher and I love you.

Thank you to my group Maddie's Minxes, your support and love for Fortis, Eidolon, and all the books I write is so important to me. Special thanks to Rowena, Tracey, Faith, Rachel, Carolyn, Kellie, Maria, Greta, Deanna, Sharon, and Linda L for making the group such a friendly place to be.

My ARC Team for not keeping me on edge too long while I wait for feedback.

A big thank you to Itsy Bitsy, and all the bloggers, authors and friends who promote my books and help others to find my books. Without you I would not be able to do this.

Lastly and most importantly thank you to my readers who have embraced my books so wholeheartedly and shown a love for the stories in my head. To hear you say that you see my characters as family makes me so humble and proud.

I hope you enjoy Gunner and Lacey as much as I did. I sure made them work for their HEA.

Author's Note

Please be aware that I use British English in my books, rather than American English so words may look different to what you are used to.

As my most of my characters are English, they also use English idioms and phrases that may seem unfamiliar to you.

If you do find something that you think is an error or typo, please email info.maddiewade@gmail.com to report it rather than using Amazon's 'report error' function. That way Amazon won't flag the book for something that could be a difference in spelling rather than an actual error.

Thanks,

Maddie   xx

I am dedicating Gunner to Tyler. I love you so much.

Prologue

Gunner tugged the mittens on, and with a final look to make sure his grandmother was busy, he slipped outside into the frigid air of the Icelandic afternoon. Running toward the lake, he breathed in the cool air, laughing when he exhaled, his breath forming patterns. Throwing out his arms, he whirled as the sense of freedom made him giddy.

He loved his amma, but she didn't understand his need to be free, to feel the sea air and the earth under him. She was old but she loved him, and he loved her, and if she didn't know she couldn't worry. She worried a lot. Milla said it was because she'd lost her child. His mother and father had died in a boating accident when he was three, but he wasn't sad because he couldn't remember them really, although that sometimes made him sad.

He had Milla though. She was his best friend and his sister. She was protective like amma was, but she let him have fun and kept his secrets—like the time he snuck onto the fishing boat they had at the dock instead of going straight home from school.

Stopping at the edge of the crystal clear water of the lake, he grinned when he saw that it had iced over since his last visit. He glanced around knowing he shouldn't go out onto the ice alone. Amma and Milla had drilled it into him time and again, but he would be fine, he was strong, and he knew this lake better than anyone.

As he tested the strength of the ice with his toe and found it had no give, he felt excitement sizzle in his blood. As he slipped and skidded, Gunner moved further out and that was when he heard his sister's voice.

"Gunner!"

He spun, hearing the anger in her voice, and as he did, he felt the ice crack beneath his feet and his heart plummeted to his belly. His arms shot out to balance himself as he stood frozen with fear.

"Milla." He heard the terror in his voice and saw the same in his big sister, but she was calm when she spoke to him.

"Gunner, stay still. I am going to come get you, okay?"

He nodded, too frightened to speak in case the sound caused the ice to crack even more. Milla went to her belly and as she inched her way out to him, he kept his eyes glued to his sister, his hero and best friend. He would never tell the boys at school that; they would make fun of him but Milla was his best friend. He dreaded the day she went to college and left him and his grandma here alone.

"Gunner, I need you to lie flat and crawl towards me."

Milla lay with her arm outstretched toward him. He felt numb with shock, his belly dipping until he thought he was going to be sick. With his legs almost frozen with fear, he began to kneel until he was belly to the ice, the cold burrowing under his clothes until his skin prickled with it or maybe it was the abject terror he was feeling. Inching forward with the slightest movements, he almost wept when his fingers brushed his sister's outstretched arm. Her eyes held his as she nodded her encouragement, and he focused everything on Milla.

"Come on, Gunner, keep going." He felt his belly lurch into his throat when the ice moved under him and he heard the frantic desperation in his sister's voice.

"Move, Gunner, now."

Her voice ringing in his ears, he crawled his way toward the shore, his breath seizing in relief when his knees hit the hard-frozen ground of land. His fright began to abate and for a split second he felt euphoria that he was okay. As Gunner spun to hug his sister and thank her, he heard the booming crack as the ice gave way. His entire world stopped in that moment as time suspended.

The smell of the air, the feel of the cool breeze on his cheeks, the way the winter sun-dappled the ice, making it shine like the most brilliant of diamonds. Most of all, he saw the look of love on Milla's face followed by the realisation that she was going under the ice and there was nothing either of them could do.

As the hiatus ceased and everything began to move at speed again, he moved to set foot on the ice.

"No!" Milla's scream made him look up as she held up her hand to stop him as the ice gave way and she sunk like a boulder beneath the frigid water. Gunner stiffened, his body refusing to move as his entire world came crashing down around him. Then his brain kicked in and his fight or flight response sprang into action as he ran for the road, screaming and waving his arms to get the attention of the fishermen heading home for the day.

More experienced than he would ever be in this situation, he watched as they quickly moved into action. Securing a blow-up dinghy to his body, one of the men rowed out over the top of the ice until he got to the gap where Milla had gone in. With the others holding the man and the dinghy secure, he slipped into the water. Gunner looked on with wild, tear-filled eyes as the seconds ticked by and still, he didn't see her, the guilt inside him a storm of destruction whirling through him as his fists clenched by his sides.

As he was about to scream his grief to the world, the man pulled Milla from the frigid lake. Her body was limp, her soaking wet hair hung over her face obscuring the smile he was desperate to see.

As the men sprang into action and pulled him to shore with an unresponsive Milla in his arms, Gunner knew that his life, and certainly Milla's life, would never be the same again and it was his fault. His selfish desire for fun had cost him his sister, his best friend, and the one person who he adored above anyone else.

Gunner sat in the hallway outside his sister's room a few days later, his head bent as he watched a spider crawl up the wall toward a web where a fly was caught. He knew how the fly felt, he was the same. He was trapped in a hell that he couldn't wake from as he saw the nightmare he'd created barrelling down on him like a freight train.

For three days he'd sat there as his grandmother spoke with doctor after doctor about his sister. He kept hearing words like vegetative state and coma and didn't know what any of it meant. All he knew was that his sister wouldn't wake up and it was his fault.

He'd done this—his selfish actions had caused it and now every time his amma looked at him all he saw was sorrow and pain. He'd hurt the two people he loved most in the world. As a strangled cry came from the room where his sister lay, he stood on the chair to try and get a better look and saw his amma on her knees as the doctor tried to comfort her. He knew the anguish and pain would stay with him until the day he died, and he deserved it.

He glanced at Milla; she had tubes coming out of her mouth, needles in her arm and her eyes were open and staring up at the ceiling. His heart hammered for a moment and he jumped down from the chair to tell his amma that Milla was awake, that everything would be okay now, but he stopped with his hand on the door at the voices inside.

"I'm so very sorry, but Milla will never be able to walk or talk or feed herself. Her brain was so damaged by the lack of oxygen that she will never recover her motor functions."

"Does she understand what is happening?" His grandmother sounded wrecked, her voice barely a whisper, gritty with distress.

"We need to run more tests, but it seems she has some cognitive thought process and recognition, but we don't know how much."

He heard footsteps come closer and quickly got back on the chair in silence, his head down to hide the tears. He didn't know what all the things the doctor had said meant but deep in his gut, he knew they were bad. As the two adults stopped at the door, the doctor lowered his voice. "My advice, Mrs Eivinsdóttir, is to find a good government assisted home and let them take care of it. The girl you know is dead and gone, and she is not coming back."

Gunner clenched his hands into fists as he listened to the hateful doctor utter those words. He was about to get up and tell the doctor he was a horrible mean man when his grandmother spoke.

"She is not an *it*. She is my granddaughter and I will care for her the same as I have always done. A person does not become expendable when they are hurt or because they can no longer do the things they once did. That, young man, is how you treat family. You care for them no matter what."

"Mrs Eivinsdóttir, I didn't mean—"

His amma cut him off. "I know what you meant, and you can forget it. Milla is my family and she's not going in a home while I'm able to look after her."

"Have you any idea of the work involved in caring for someone with her special needs? It is a twenty-four hour, seven days a week task."

"I don't care, she's family."

Gunner heard the masculine sigh as the door was pulled open and the doctor looked down at him as Gunner glared at him with defiance.

"You have no idea what you have caused, do you, child?" The doctor shook his head as he walked away and Gunner fought the tears that stung the back of his nose, the guilt like an anvil he thought he might never stand again the burden was so heavy.

A strong arm came around him and he leaned into his grandmother's familiar hold, taking comfort he didn't deserve. The

7

man might be mean, but he was right. This was his fault and he would do whatever it took to ease the burden his reckless behaviour had placed on his amma. As for Milla, that was something he would have to live with. It would be his penance for the life he'd stolen from her. He would live for both of them, do the things she'd dreamed of and serve those who needed him. But he would never again let anyone in. He wasn't worthy of love and loving someone made you open to the pain that he now felt as he cried against his grandmother's   shoulder.

Chapter 1

Lacey hated airports; she'd spent so much time in them throughout her career that she was over the whole experience. Looking up at the screens where the flights were listed, she groaned in frustration as the times all began to flick over to read delayed. That was just her luck, to be stranded in Düsseldorf International Airport overnight because of some damn storm.

Lacey sighed as she sank onto the hard-plastic seats made for torture and tried to decide what to do next. She was meant to be on her way to Gatwick where her friends Skye and Nate were picking her up. Lacey took out her phone and shot a text to Skye to let her know that the flight was delayed, and she would call when she knew more.

Putting her phone back in her Radley handbag, which was one of her favourite extravagances, she looked around the lounge as she figured out her next move. She should probably book herself a room overnight as the hotels would book up fast now with all flights off the table.

Rushing to the desk, she was glad she'd packed a few essentials in her hand luggage, the rest she could get at one of the shops in the terminal building. Seeing the pretty brunette woman at the desk, she smiled her best 'please be nice smile' and hoped she got lucky.

"Hi, can you help me? I need to book a room in the closest hotel."

In heavily accented English the woman began to explain that a lot of the hotels were booked because there was some exhibition in town. Lacey felt her heart sink at the thought of a night in the airport on a chair.

"I don't mind what it is, but can you try?"

With a huff, the woman began to type on her screen and then picked up the phone and called someone. She began speaking in rapid German, which sounded like she was telling someone off as she looked Lacey over as if she was an irritating fly she wanted to stamp on.

"Name?"

"Lacey Cannon."

Lacey bit her lip and kept silent, hoping her compliance would win her brownie points. The woman eventually put the phone down and looked at her with a bored expression.

"You have a room booked at the Sheraton."

Lacey's legs almost gave way with relief; she was bone tired and just wanted a bed for the night.

"Thank you so much."

As Lacey thanked her, the desk attended finally smiled, and it completely transformed her harsh features. It was one of the things Lacey knew from her modelling days, yet so many designers wanted them all to remain impassive and expressionless, like the mannequins they really were. It was something she wouldn't allow in her children's clothing line. All her kids had fun when they modelled, whether that was on the runway or behind a camera.

As she pulled her coat closer and stepped outside, the wind whipped her light blonde hair across her face. The storm was set to hit later tonight with gale-force winds and torrential rain for the next twenty-four hours.

Lifting a hand, she waved down a cab to the Sheraton. Once there, she tipped the driver and then checked in, noting the hotel had a spa pool and a cocktail bar. As she eyed the hotel shop, she realised she'd need to buy a swimsuit as hers was packed and on the plane.

The room was beautiful as Lacey had known it would be, but she'd stayed in a hundred different rooms like it in her time, and as elegant as it was, she craved a home of her own. A place she could decorate and plant flowers and get a cat if she wanted. Roots. She wanted roots and a family, but for now, she'd settle for her own place.

Dumping her bags in the bedroom, she grabbed her purse and went down to the gift shop and picked out a red swimsuit with a cute little belt and added some personal items before paying. As she exited the shop, she realised her tiredness had disappeared, and she sighed knowing another night of insomnia was in her future unless she could tire herself out with swimming, and if not, there was always the hotel bar.

Quickly she changed and stowed her clothes and purse in the locker before wrapping her hair in a ponytail and walked into the almost empty pool area. Her breath left her in a sigh, and she wondered if she would ever get over her wariness of strangers. Yet, even as she thought it, she knew it wasn't the strangers that had caused damage to her psyche but the man who was meant to have loved her.

Shaking off the heavyweight of melancholy that hit her, she replaced it with the kind eyes of the Viking warrior who'd saved her. She knew he wasn't a Viking but with his long blond hair, blue eyes, and muscular build, he could've been. Especially with his sexy accent that hinted at a Swedish or Icelandic birth.

She knew from talking to Skye, Gunner was no longer working for Eidolon, but she didn't know what the story was and had forced herself not to ask. Obsessing over a man she couldn't have and shouldn't be attracted to was utter stupidity. Gunner was too much man for her. She should've learned her lesson going for alpha males, it never worked out, and the last one had nearly killed her.

No, the only man in her future was her godson Noah, and maybe if she met a nice bookish professor, that could work. Placing her towel on a lounger, she walked to the edge and dove into the clear, cold water and began to swim laps. Her body and mind focused on each stroke as she swam lap after lap, not stopping to rest. Swimming was her relaxation, the way she kept her body toned and fit. Lacey hated to exercise, but she loved to swim, and if a modelling agency hadn't picked her up, her coach said she could've gone to the Olympics. Lacey wasn't sure about that, but she did love it, and it was a moot point now anyway.

After one hundred laps, she stopped to catch her breath and evaluate her muscles. They were aching, but she thought she could keep going, that was when she spotted a man watching her from the doorway. She couldn't see his face, but she knew deep in her bones he was watching her, and it made the fine hairs on her neck stand on end in warning.

After what happened with her ex, when he'd kidnapped her at Nate and Skye's wedding reception, she'd learned to listen to her gut, and it was telling her to leave this area and go someplace open.

Hauling herself from the pool, she grabbed her towel and quickly wrapped it around her body before walking into the ladies changing rooms. She smiled at two women who were chatting in German as they changed and slid into a private cubicle after retrieving her bag.

In minutes she'd dressed and pulled her blonde hair into a ponytail high on her head to keep the wet strands off her neck.

Stepping from the beautifully decorated spa, she looked around the lobby of the hotel for anyone who might spark her fight or flight response and found nobody of interest. Shaking it off with a nervous laugh at her own paranoia, Lacey spotted the bar. That was what she needed—a drink to relax her and help her sleep.

With that decided she headed upstairs to drop off her bag, dismissing her earlier worries. As she took the elevator up, it stopped on the floor below her own and a man she didn't know or recognise got in with a smile. He was handsome in a custom-fitted suit from one of her favourite designers. His eyes moved over her from head to toe in a silent invitation that made her body react but not in the way she'd expected. There was no desire, only the intrinsic need to run as she saw the cold in his eyes touch her.

Chapter 2

It was typical of his fucking luck for a storm to blow in now of all times and derail his plans to give Jack the answers he'd been holding back from him for over two years. Gunner looked in the mirror of his hotel bathroom and saw nothing of the man who'd signed on with Eidolon.

Hope was a fragile emotion that he should've known better than to feel. Yet he had, even after he vowed never to hope again after his sister was injured because of his own selfishness. He'd thought that joining the British Air Force and climbing his way into a good job, one that fed his injured soul enough that he could bury the bitter grief and guilt he still carried.

But even flying every aircraft known to man hadn't extinguished the burn in the pit of his stomach every time he saw his sister in the facility he paid for. Her life had ended that day on the lake, in every way that mattered anyway. He'd been going through the motions until he met Jack, and he'd offered him the opportunity to do more.

Gunner had jumped at the chance and loved his place in Eidolon, genuinely feeling for the first time in his life like he belonged. The men he served with became the brothers he'd never had, giving him a family again.

Then it had all come to a screeching halt one day when he'd opened his door to a man who'd brought reality crashing in on him like a freight train. He'd had one choice to make, and as he looked at the haunted, dead eyes in the mirror, he knew it had been the wrong one.

He'd chosen to betray his friends to save his sister, to break a bond forged in blood because he could not face the way they would look at him when they found out what he'd done to Milla, and to protect the man who had offered him hope from the truth.

Now they knew about his sister anyway, and the ties that had almost dragged him free were now the same ones that would pull him under. The loss of his family at his own hand had shaped him into the man he was today, but the way he'd betrayed his friends was the legacy he now had to live with.

Splashing cold water on his face, he watched the droplets slide down the stubble of his chin, exhaustion a constant companion these days. At least Milla was safe now, another debt he owed Eidolon and would never be able to repay.

Pulling his long hair back into a band at the back of his head, he walked from the bathroom and threw on a clean white t-shirt. He checked his phone and saw he had a message from Bás confirming the men he was meant to meet were also delayed, and the meeting would now take place in two days' time.

Gunner wasn't a fool, he knew the risks he took going to this meeting, but it was the least he owed Jack. To give them the truth and open up the lies and treason that was at the centre of everything. Handing Jack the truth was all he had left to give now, and if it cost him his life, he didn't care. In fact, at this point, it would be favourable to the life he was forced to live now.

He was tired, so bone-tired of fighting, and he had so many regrets that he could hardly breathe from the weight of them. A vision popped into his head of Lacey Cannon, the woman they'd rescued from her psycho ex when he'd kidnapped her at Skye and Nate's wedding. In another life, he would've asked her out, spent some time with her, maybe even fallen in love with the blonde beauty, but that wasn't on the cards for him.

Needing to get out of this room before he went stir crazy, he grabbed his wallet, phone, and key card and headed for the elevator and the bar he'd spotted downstairs. A few drinks might help relax him enough to sleep, failing that, he'd drink until he passed out cold.

Hitting the button, he waited as he watched the numbers move before his impatience got the better of him, and he decided to take the stairs, his gun tucked into his leg holster out of sight. Never leaving the room unarmed was something Jack and Alex had drilled into them. The gun laws in the UK, of course, didn't allow people to carry guns but they had a special licence, and although he no longer had that he still carried everywhere, he went. Especially as he had a target on his back now.

His long legs ate up the steps as he jogged downstairs and out into the foyer of the hotel. He walked past the lift and saw it was still stuck on the same floor, making him glad he'd walked.

The bar was more of a cocktail lounge with a piano in the corner that matched the one he'd seen in the lobby of the hotel. It had a certain nineteen forties vibe that he liked, and as he ordered himself a beer from the bartender with the handlebar moustache, his fingers itched to play.

Taking the beer, he pointed at the piano with a question, and the bartender nodded for him to go ahead. Gunner sat at the black grand piano and placed his drink on the floor beside him. It had been a long time since he'd played but his grandmother had insisted it was the one thing he kept up, even after Milla was injured. She'd said it nurtured his sensitive soul and the thought made him smile.

The time he'd spent with her practising was among only a handful of happy memories he had. His hand caressed the ivories with reverence, the feel of calm he always had when he played was the same as when he flew—pure peace. Everything else ceased to exist for him when he played. He began to play, and all the pain and tension left him as his fingers moved over the keys. 'River Flows' by Yiruma was one of his sister's favourites, and he closed his eyes as the music washed over him.

He was halfway through the piece when he realised someone else was playing the same music as him from the piano in the lobby. He couldn't see the person, but he heard the music and increased his tempo slightly, seeing if they would keep up and he was happy when they did. People began to drift toward him to watch as others moved to the lobby to see who played with him.

He should stop, he knew that his job was to be a ghost, but this was the first time in a long time he'd felt alive, and he didn't want to give it up. So, he kept going, faster and faster they played until the culmination of the piece peaked and then slowed as the duet ended with the last haunting note.

Gunner was on his feet as soon as the last note played, his interest piqued as to the identity of his duet partner. He rounded the corner and came slap bang into the one woman he thought never to see again. A woman who'd played the lead in many a fantasy and it felt like fate that she'd be here now.

"Lacey?"

"Gunner?"

"What are you doing here?"

She moved closer, closing the gap between them and the scent of her hit him like a punch to the gut. She looked stunning, her eyes bright, skin flawless, the wounded look he'd last seen in her eyes after her kidnapping almost gone.

"I had a flight cancelled because of the storm."

He stepped up beside her as they moved into the bar area. "Drink?"

"Yes, please. I was headed here when I heard someone playing and couldn't resist joining in. It's one of my favourite pieces."

"No way, me too."

Lacey cocked her head as she hitched up onto a barstool. "That was you?"

Gunner nodded. "Yep."

"Wow, you are a dark horse. Are you here because of the storm too?"

Gunner asked for another beer and motioned for her to order what she wanted, not surprised when she got a Cosmo and added it to his tab.

"Yes, I have a meeting."

He motioned to a table in the corner, wanting to spend this time with her, seizing it for what it was; a prize when he needed it most. He followed behind, his eyes falling to the sexy curves of her ass in the tight jeans she wore with sky-high heels. Her hair was wet and in a simple ponytail, and it made her look young, innocent, and fucking beautiful.

He dragged his eyes up as they sat down but knew he'd been caught checking her out as he sat and saw the raised eyebrow she gave him. Gunner grinned and shrugged. "Can't blame me for looking."

"I wasn't. I just wondered if you'd give me the same chance." Her flirty tone was one he remembered from the wedding before her attack. He smirked and lifted his drink with a wink that made her blush a pretty shade of pink.

"So, tell me about you. How have you been? What's the gossip?"

Gunner sputtered. "Gossip? Do I look like a man who gossips?"

"No, men are useless at gossip, but it was worth a try. I hear you left Eidolon."

Gunner felt his body go rigid. "Who told you that?"

He saw Lacey rear back at the sharp snap of his tone and regretted it instantly.

16

"Nate said you weren't there anymore, but that's all he said. Look, Gunner, if you'd rather not talk about it, then that's fine. I'm the Queen of self-denial and know better than anyone about privacy and how sacred it is."

Her response and understanding had him wanting to kick his own ass. "I'm sorry. I was a dick. Forgive me?"

"Fine, so let's talk about something else. Who taught you to play like that?"

Gunner felt himself relax in the easy way she acquiesced to his request. "My grandmother, she made me practise every day from the time I was six until the day I left home to join the military."

"Same, but for me, it was my mother. I'm actually glad she did, the piano is such a relaxing thing to play. Other than swimming, it's one of my favourite things to do."

"You like to swim?"

"Yep, I nearly went pro, but then I got scouted, and the rest, as they say, is history."

"Flying is like that for me, all the shit in your head is silent. I love it. The freedom, the quiet, you can hear yourself think." He looked away when he saw her looking at him and realised he'd given away more than he wanted. "So, what has you heading to the UK? Are you headed to visit Skye and Nate?"

Lacey held his gaze as she sipped her drink. "Actually, I'm relocating to Hereford."

"Wow really? That's great, good for you."

"Yeah, I'm excited. I get to be close to my best friend and my godchildren, and I have contacts there and a few friends too."

"That's wonderful, Lacey. I'm pleased for you."

He watched her run her finger over the condensation on her glass, her movements lazy, unhurried, and he wondered what she would do if he leaned in and did that to her neck with his tongue. Probably slap him across the face. "What about you, will you be there?"

Chapter 3

Regret was a bitter taste in his mouth as he focused on her question and realised he would likely be dead before too long, and for the first time in a long while he wished things were different. "No, I won't be there. My life is on a different path now." He didn't say anything else, and she didn't ask.

"Hey, do you want to play a drinking game?" She grinned, and the sudden way she changed direction on him had laughter bubbling up in his belly.

"Sure, why not? We're not going anywhere for a bit."

"Okay, let's play never have I ever. I'll say something I've never done, and if you've done it, you take a drink, and we take it in turns. Okay?"

"Yep, all set. Let's get some shots and make this interesting." He called the waitress over and ordered another round of beers and cosmos and some tequila shots. When they had their drinks, he lifted his pint glass for her to go.

"Never have I ever jumped out of a plane."

Gunner took a drink. "That's cheating. You know what I do for a job."

"I don't make the rules, Viking."

He chuckled at her calling him Viking, remembering she had at the wedding too and he'd liked it then as much as he did now, even after explaining Vikings came from Norway, not Iceland.

"Never have I ever walked a catwalk."

Lacey took a drink and her turn. "Never have I ever sung karaoke."

Gunner shook his head.

"Never have I ever been to the hairdressers."

He saw her surprised look as she drank again and he had a feeling he might win this game but after a few more rounds where she drank twice what he did, she changed things up.

"Never have I ever swum naked in the sea."

Gunner felt his balls tighten at the thought of Lacey naked. He saw the challenge in her blue eyes that had gone lazy with desire. He took a large drink to give his brain time to calm down and erase the

18

image of her lush body dripping wet as she stood in the sea like a siren.

"Never have I ever watched Fifty Shades of Grey."

He grinned as she drank.

"Never have I ever sent a naked selfie to someone."

He shrugged and didn't drink. He wasn't a fool, but his dick was definitely interested in this game and the thought of her taking naked selfies.

"Never have I ever had phone sex."

His eyes brows shot up when she threw back a shot, and he had to adjust his jeans as his dick went from slightly keen to straining against his zipper.

"Never have I ever been tied up in bed."

Jesus fucking Christ she was going to kill him. He'd never been tied up so didn't drink.

"Never have I ever said I love you."

Lacey drank as he'd known she would, and he saw her leaning sideways on her chair. He was almost double her weight, so was always going to win this game, but he had to admit it was the most fun he'd had in a very long time. He couldn't deny that the thought she'd said I love you to someone made him feel all kinds of jealous which was crazy considering they were nothing to each other and never would be now.

"Never have I ever brought myself to climax in front of someone."

Gunner almost choked and took a drink to clear his throat and then realised it looked like he'd done it when he hadn't.

"I never have, but fuck, woman, the images you're putting in my head are dangerous."

"Yeah." Her words were slurring as she closed an eye to try and focus. This evening was coming to an end, and he didn't want it to.

"Think perhaps we should get you back to your room?" He stood and made his way around the table to Lacey, who was wavering back and forth in her chair. He hooked her under her arms, and she leaned on him; her breast brushed his arm, and he tried not to groan out loud.

"I think that is a good idea, Viking." Gunner chuckled which wasn't something he'd anticipated on this trip at all.

He got her to the lift, and once inside, she curled into him, her head in his neck, her lips resting against his pulse. He wasn't a dick, but he was a human, and she was testing every ounce of control he had with her sweet mouth on him. Just the thought of those lips around his cock had him having to adjust his jeans so he didn't end up with permanent teeth marks from the zipper.

Lacey was the one woman he hadn't been able to get out of his head, and yet they'd barely shared a kiss. He didn't know what it was about her, but she'd burrowed into his soul and made a place for herself there. Had life been different, he would've followed up after her attack, made sure she was safe, that she was recovering and maybe even asked her out on a date.

Yet that wasn't his path now, the choices he'd made had steered him in a direction he couldn't come back from. Up until a few hours ago, he didn't even care if he came out of this alive. His only focus to end the threat to his former team and his family, and if he died doing it, he was okay with that.

He looked down at the woman who was snuggled against his side as he walked her to her door and wished things were different, that he was a better man. Her scent played havoc with his control as she struggled to find her key card in her bag. Gently he took it from her fingers and unlocked her door for her, pushing the door open wide.

As he did, his instincts kicked in as he saw the destruction inside. A gasp of dismay had him pulling Lacey behind him at the same time he pulled his weapon.

"Stay here. I need to check and make sure nobody is still in there."

Lacey nodded, all signs of her drunken state seeming to have fled to be replaced by fear.

Gunner cleared each room silently and efficiently, stepping over her clothes strewn about the bedroom, the mattress that had been slashed, and the tv smashed on the floor. Whoever had done this had been frenzied, but they were gone now. Quickly he made his way back to Lacey, who was standing exactly where he'd left her by the door. Her skin was paler than usual, her eyes bright with fear instead of the joy and desire of moments ago, and for that alone, Gunner wanted to rip whoever had done this to shreds.

20

Taking her arm, he led her out of the room and back towards the elevator, hitting the button for his floor. Lacey was quiet as if she was in shock, and he knew this would be bringing back unhappy memories for her. As the doors opened, she seemed to snap out of her fog.

"Where are we going?"

Gunner took her upper arm in his hand and directed her toward his room. "My room. We can call security from there."

"Oh, okay."

He didn't like that placid acceptance from her, not because it wasn't helpful but because her fire was integral to her personality. Not in the same way Pax or Evelyn had fire, hers was more subtle, refined.

Moving into the room, he checked his own security measures were in place, and happy his room hadn't been breached, he took her inside and led her toward the couch. She sat with a shiver, and he crouched down and pulled a blanket from the back of the sofa over her shoulders.

"Thank you."

Her voice was small, and he had to grit his teeth to bite back the growl in his throat. Leaning forward, he kissed her forehead, needing to touch her in some way, to reassure her she wasn't alone. His brain was running scenarios as to who had done this. Was this to do with him or her previous boyfriend or merely a robbery?

Stepping to the fridge, he grabbed two bottles of water, figuring they'd probably had enough alcohol for tonight. He offered her one, and she took it with shaking hands and trepid smile.

"I need to make some calls. You okay for a minute?" Lacey nodded, and he was relieved to see some of the colour coming back into her cheeks. Gunner moved to the other side of the room and took out his phone. He had a choice to make now. Did he call Bás or Jack? It wasn't much of a choice he realised as he dialled the number and waited.

"Yes?"

"Jack, it's Gunner."

Gunner could practically hear his former boss sit up straighter. "What's wrong?" One of Jack's many talents was being able to read people's voices and now was no different.

"I'm in Düsseldorf at the Sheraton. My flight got cancelled."

"And this concerns me because?"

"I ran into Lacey Cannon and we had a drink. When I walked her back to her room. We found it had been trashed. All her things slashed, mattress slashed, the whole works."

"Is she okay?"

"Yeah, a little shaken up but she's fine. I'm going to call security as soon as we hang up." Gunner sighed and rubbed his temples where a headache was forming. "I know I have no right to ask favours from you, but could you get in touch with Nate and see if Fortis can look into her ex and see if he's still in prison?"

"I can do that. Anything else?"

"Make sure Nate meets her at the airport. I can keep an eye on her here, but if this is somehow connected to me, I don't want her left alone."

"You think it is?"

"Not really, but enough people have gotten hurt because of me. I won't let her become another victim."

"Consider it done."

Jack hung up, and Gunner felt the knot of tension in his belly ease. Now he had to get Lacey safely into the hands of Nate and Fortis, and she'd be fine. Like Eidolon, Fortis Security consisted of former Special Forces that were more like family than anything else. He knew Zack and his team would make sure the woman who was looking at him like he had all the answers safe. Gunner scoffed silently as he called the front desk. He didn't have answers, and the truth was, he'd made such a fuck up of his life he could hardly find his face in the mirror these days.

But by God, he'd keep her safe if it killed him.

Chapter 4

Lacey could feel the effects of the alcohol wearing off already and was glad to have her head clearer. The small visual she'd seen of her room before he'd ushered her out of there had been like a dagger to the heart. Her sense of security had vanished in the blink of an eye. Her damaged clothes and personal items were all replaceable, piece of mind wasn't. All the techniques she'd put in place after her attack by her ex-lover, Carmine Russo, were gone as fear overwhelmed her in a heartbeat.

Lacey looked up as Gunner moved to sit next to her, his body providing warmth and comfort as he lifted his arm and she scooted closer to feel the safety of his body close to hers. He leaned them back on the couch, and she settled against him with a trust she'd always felt for this man. He was a protector, and she knew he'd never let anyone harm her while he was around.

Lacey also knew it was temporary. Whatever forces had brought them together were fleeting, and she mourned that fact above all others.

"How are you doing, Cosmo?"

Lacey felt her lips tip up at the new nickname. "Better, thank you." She knew she should be dealing with this herself, not allowing Gunner to swoop in and be the hero. She needed to be her own hero and take back control. That had been the thing that kept her sane after Carmine had held her at gunpoint and tried to force her to marry him. A rigid control on her life and her future. It was one of the reasons she was moving to Hereford and leaving the city.

A home of her own surrounded by people who made her feel safe would give her that. Having her own business and not relying on managers and agents gave her more control, but for this one minute she needed to lean on someone, and Gunner was the man she trusted to hold her while she shored up her emotional defences.

A short time later a knock on the door had her stiffening and siting up sharply, her muscles tensing for flight. Gunner's hand on her cheek, forced her to look up at him, anchored her to the moment. "It's hotel security."

Lacey nodded, feeling foolish. Gunner moved to the door, checking before he let the man in, conversing with him in flawless German. Gunner moved back to her and crouched in front of her, his hand landing on her knee and rubbing in a circular motion meant to ease her.

"Apparently, the security footage shows a man going into your room shortly after you left, but a cap obscures his face. They want to know if you saw anything suspicious in the hallway?"

Lacey stopped, remembering the feeling of being watched as she swam, and the man in the elevator who'd given her the creeps but had done nothing to her other than that. Lacey rolled her lips, considering how to say it without sounding like some paranoid female.

Gunner angled his head, and she could tell he knew she was hiding something. "Lacey?"

"I got the feeling someone was watching me when I took my swim earlier, and then in the lift on the way down to the bar, some guy gave me the creeps, but he didn't do or say anything to me."

"Fuck, Lacey, why didn't you tell me?"

Lacey's spine stiffened at his sharp tone, and she went still under his hand. "Why the hell would I have told you, Gunner? We're nothing to each other, barely even friends."

She saw her words wound the gentle giant of a man as he nodded. "Fair point. Can you give me any more details?"

"Gunner, I'm sorry, I didn't mean that. Of course we're friends. You saved me once before and again tonight. I can never repay that. I'm a little edgy, but that doesn't excuse me being a bitch."

His crooked grin hit her right in the belly, forming a warmth to permeate her body in the most intimate places. Damn this man was attractive, she'd felt the physical pull when they'd first met and again tonight.

"You could never be bitchy, Cosmo. I shouldn't have reacted as I did. You owe me nothing."

"I owe you so much more than that. You're my saviour yet again." Her words had the opposite effect of what she wanted, and she saw him pull down emotional walls right in front of her. His expressive blue eyes went hard, his jaw a stone mask on his handsome face.

"I'm nobody's saviour."

24

With that he stood and went and spoke to the security officer, she guessed relaying her answers to him. The next half hour was spent recounting every detail from tonight to security and then for a few hours after that, the German police.

As Gunner closed the door, she was regarding him warily. He'd relaxed a little but was still maintaining his distance, and she hated it. She wanted the relaxed, warm man from earlier who had played the piano and then flirted over drinking games with her, but she had no clue how to reach him.

"You can stay here tonight. I'll take the couch."

She should argue, but the truth was she felt safer when he was around. He'd taken a call earlier to say her ex-boyfriend was still locked up, so there was that at least.

"I can take the couch," she began but stopped when he arched a brow at her. "Come on. I'm half the size of you."

"Don't give a rats ass if you're a fucking faerie. You're taking the bed. If anything comes through that door, there's no way in hell you're between it and me." He shook his head, emphatically. "No fucking way."

"Fine. Alright if I take a shower first?"

Gunner grunted, and she took it as a yes and shut the door to the bathroom. The hot shower made her feel more human as the last of the booze wore off, leaving her with just the come down from the shock of the evening. Slipping on a t-shirt Gunner had given her, she towel-dried her hair and then cracked the bedroom door allowing the light from the lounge to creep in and light the dark corners.

It was embarrassing to admit that as a grown-ass woman, she was scared of the dark, but it was the truth. Sliding into the bed that Gunner should have been using, she curled on her side and tried to shut out all the memories that tried to weaken her from flooding her mind.

Instead, she let her mind wander to the memory of Gunner's arms around her as she listened to him quietly walking about the other room. It made her feel safe enough to fall into a fitful sleep.

The next thing she knew, arms were around her and an absent screaming was hurting her ears as she fought the invisible foe off with little effect.

"Lacey, hey, it's me." The deep voice managed to get through the fog of terror and the sound of screaming eased until she realised it had been her. With a sob, she fell into Gunner's arms realising she'd had another dream. It had been six months since the last, and she'd thought she was winning this silent battle with her demons but evidently, the robbery tonight had set her back.

Wiping her eyes with the tissue Gunner offered, she fought to pull her shit together until she was somewhat under control again. Chancing a glance at Gunner she saw nothing but compassion and a steely determination to protect on his gorgeous face.

"I'm okay now."

"I'm glad you are, Cosmo. Damn near gave me a heart attack." He flopped back on the bed, pulling her in close as she held tight.

"Sorry. I thought I was over them, but it looks like the nightmares are back."

Gunner stroked her hair, and she realised he was in only athletic shorts as her fingers touched the warm muscle of his chest.

"Don't apologise, Lacey. I, more than anyone, know how real nightmares can be."

"You have them?"

"I did. Sometimes I still do."

"Do you remember them?" Her fingers skimmed over his skin, making him shiver, the muscle rippling with strength.

"Every detail."

He went silent, and she wondered if he would tell her but stayed quiet, not wanting him to bring his walls back up. She was sure he wouldn't answer when he began to speak, his voice low, the pain like cut glass on her skin.

"I have a sister."

Not what Lacey was expecting, but she stayed silent, knowing that this was important.

"Milla is seven years older than me, always protected me but she was my best friend. When my parents died, I was only three, so didn't remember them much. Milla sheltered me. We had my grandmother, who was a saint to be looking after two kids but losing a child had made her nervous, so she was strict. She hated me doing anything dangerous in her mind, and so I hid it. Milla was the buffer and let me get away with so much." His chuckle was humourless as it faded away. Lacey felt the overpowering need to comfort this man who had saved her, to take away his pain.

"You don't have to go on if it's too painful."

"I went out onto the lake when I shouldn't have, and it started to crack. Milla, she came out after me and got me to safety, but the ice was too thin, and she went in the water. By the time they got her out, her brain had been starved of oxygen for too long. She has a brain injury, locked in a body and mind that won't work anymore, and it's my fault."

The anguish broke her heart as tears for this warrior, and everything he'd lost, fell down her cheeks and onto his warm skin.

Bringing her hand up, she angled his face toward her and saw the pain in the ice-blue depths. "You were a child."

"I should have known better."

"Maybe but all kids do things they know they shouldn't, but not all of them end up with such horrific consequences. You take the blame, but it was her choice not to get help, her choice to go after you. Do you really think she would want you to blame yourself for what happened?" Gunner stayed still lost in his own guilt, and for the first time, she saw a man on the edge. Weighed down by guilt and pain that she didn't fully understand and more than anything she wanted to take away his pain.

Without thinking, she pulled his head down, seeing the fire in his eyes return before her lips touched his. Firm and gentle, she kissed him until her tongue flicked at his closed lips and then he took over. He rolled them so he covered her body with his own, his big hands cupping her face as he kissed his way down her neck, desire and need taking over them both as each touch became frenzied and desperate.

His teeth grazed her neck, and she moaned with a burst of pleasure as her nails found his back, scoring along the warm skin making him groan as he rocked his hard length against her core until she was mewling, the orgasm just out of reach. Gunner pulled away, lifting his tee over her head until she lay beneath him in her underwear. His eyes feasted on her like she was precious.

As a model, Lacey felt confident having eyes on her body, but the tenderness and awe she saw in Gunner's eyes made her desperate to feel everything with him. Slipping her hand into his shorts, she grasped his hard length and stroked as he groaned and pumped his hips into her hand.

"Fuck, Cosmo, you're going to kill me."

"I want you, Gunner." Never in her life had she wanted anything more than she wanted to feel this man inside her. His lips found hers as his fingers toyed with her swollen clit, making her arch into him as she pushed his shorts down the thick muscles of his thighs.

Sliding her panties down her legs, she kicked them off as he wrapped her leg around his waist, and she felt the tip of him against her entrance. His lips on her nipple as he sucked first one tip and then the other into his mouth, driving her crazy with lust, had her almost coming undone in his arms.

But his fingers on her clit stroking her to a fever pitch as she urged him closer made her gasp as her climax hit her in a wave of pleasure so intense, she couldn't catch her breath. Pulses of bliss spasmed through her body like fireworks as he continued to lavish her body with his wickedly good hands.

"So beautiful, Cosmo." His words were ragged as he nipped and kissed her mouth and neck.

"I want to feel you inside me."

"Are you sure?"

Lacey grasped his long hair by the roots and forced his eyes to her. "Fuck me, Gunner."

His lazy smile was not what she expected, but a second later as he pushed his hard cock inside her, all other thoughts fled her brain.

Everything from the unfamiliar burn of him stretching her body, to the feeling of being full was perfect. She held on to the silky strands of his hair as he gazed down at her, tension bracketing every nuance of his face and she knew he was worried he'd hurt her.

"I need you to move, Gunner."

He wasted no more words but did as she asked, they quickly reached a rhythm that neither could control. Passion driving them both towards climax as hands touched and mouths kissed and licked until they were both wild, out of control, and it felt good. So good Lacey gripped his shoulders in fear she would splinter from the pleasure.

"Hold on to me, Lacey. I won't let you fall."

His words, the tender way he was protecting her even now, threw her over the edge as her body tightened and she felt him swell inside her and then he was with her, his movements jerky as he filled her with his seed and that was when the reality hit.

They hadn't used protection.

His eyes moved up to her face, and she saw the truth in his eyes. They'd been so caught up, neither one of them had thought about anything other than the need driving them. A need that was no less there, not now that she knew what it felt like to be fucked by this brutal, gentle, man.

"I'm so sorry."

The guilt on his face almost broke her heart. She didn't know Gunner well, but she felt like she did. His history with his sister was only a part of why he looked so lonely and lost, there was more too it. She just hoped she got the chance to find out the rest.

As he pulled out of her, she felt an empty sense of loss in her belly as his walls came back down. Silently he walked to the bathroom and got a cloth to clean them both up, not letting her help when she reached for the cloth but tending to her himself. How could this man not see himself for what he was—a protector.

Lacey was surprised when he got in beside her and pulled her into his arms, expecting him to run from the intimacy.

"I'm clean."

"Me too." She hesitated over her next words, not quite sure how to tell him that tonight could have far-reaching consequences that neither one of them had been expecting.

"I'm not on the pill." Lacey could hear every single sound in the room as the silence became deafening, yet he didn't flinch or scream and shout at her, Gunner just held her.

"Whatever happens, we'll face it together. I won't let you down, Lacey."

"Thank you."

The words felt insignificant to her own ears, but they were all she had. It had been so long since she'd faced anything with someone having her back that she didn't know how to express it. Not because she didn't have people who loved her, but because keeping her anxiety quiet had become the norm to her.

"Don't thank me, Cosmo, this should never have happened in the first place."

Lacey tensed, angry that he would say something like that about an experience she knew she would treasure for the rest of her life whatever the outcome.

"I'm sorry you feel that way." Yet even as she spoke, she snuggled closer to him, and he held her tighter.

When Lacey woke the next morning, she knew he was gone, the cold sheets beside her evidence of that and the tears pricked for just a moment until she saw the note by the bed and realised he'd been true to his word.

Chapter 5

He'd always known he was a bastard but sleeping with Lacey without using protection was a new low, even for him. Gunner had left her in bed, knowing that if he stayed, he'd make love to her again. The attraction between them was too strong, and after his confession about his sister, he'd been too raw to resist what she was offering.

Even now as he watched her from afar, he didn't know why he'd told her about Milla when he'd never told another living soul about her. Ever since yesterday morning when he'd walked away, leaving her with just a note to say he'd be in touch, he'd been watching.

Part of it was he needed to know she was safe; the other part was because he just couldn't seem to help himself. He was up to his neck in danger, with threats around every corner and coming from multiple directions, and yet, all he'd done all day was observe her every move to make sure she was safe.

Now he watched her go through the gate to board the flight to the UK where Nate would make sure she was safe. He felt the knot in his belly ease that she was away from the menace of his life even as his chest ached with the thought of her so far away from him.

Shaking his head, he spun on his heel and jogged to his own gate to catch the short flight to Nuremberg. He had a job to do, and if he had any hope of surviving it, he had to get his head in the game. He would be meeting Deputy Director Osbourne to provide security for a meeting with his partner, whose identity he was still unsure of. This partner was facilitating an introduction to a contact called Samir al-Sadir.

Sadir had just turned twenty-one and was a sick son of bitch who was taking over the reins from his dead father, Miqdaad al-Sadir. Sadir was a drug lord, embedded in the foothills of Parwan Province in Afghanistan.

Eidolon had taken out Miqdaad and his network on one of their very first missions, and until recently he hadn't known why, happy to know that there was one less asshole out there selling drugs and weapons.

Now he knew the real reason Miqdaad had to die, and it had been one of the reasons he'd chosen to betray Eidolon. Every second of that betrayal tasted like bile in his mouth as he thought of the things he'd done, not only to protect Milla but also to protect the man who'd been like a brother to him from a truth that would break him.

Eidolon and the men who'd become family to him were so much more than a Ghost Ops team. They protected the very fabric of the British Monarchy, handling missions straight from the hand of the Queen. A woman who was fair and kind and loved her people and her country unreservedly. Gunner had come to love his home country more than the wild beauty of his birth one—the memories of that hostile allure too painful for him.

Slipping headphones on his head, he settled back in his seat for the four-hour flight and closed his eyes. But he didn't sleep, his mind playing over every moment he'd spent with Lacey both now and at Nate and Skye's wedding. She'd changed since her attack, grown stronger but also more reserved. Yet with him, she'd been the woman he'd first met, comfortable to smile, confident and sure. Yet, as he pictured her even then, he knew she'd been hiding pain.

If he could go back and hurt Carmine Russo for what he'd done to Lacey, he would in a heartbeat. He didn't give a shit about turning the other cheek or being the better man; he'd pummel the snot out of him.

As he disembarked, he grabbed the hand luggage from the overhead locker. Gunner kept his eyes peeled for Bás who should be there already and picking him up. Making his way outside, he felt the man who was even now a mystery to him, step up beside him, appearing from nowhere.

"Heard you had a spot of bother at the hotel in Düsseldorf."

Gunner climbed in the back seat of the car and glanced at Bás who settled beside him. The guy in the front was one of the usual drivers who was more brawn than brain, but Gunner kept his answer vague anyway.

"Not really, just a damsel in distress."

"You sure about that?"

Gunner knew what he was asking. If Gunner lost focus on this mission because of a woman, a body bag would be the only way he went home, and that was if there was enough of a body to bury. The thought hadn't bothered him before, but now with the chance, however slight, that Lacey could be carrying his child, he had the desire to live more than ever before. He wouldn't divulge that to the man beside him though, that was his to know, and his trust in the man only went so far. He knew more than anyone you couldn't trust anyone.

"What is the plan for the meet?"

Bás cocked his head but let whatever was on his mind go and focused on the task at hand. Gunner had no clue what his end game was, but currently, it aligned with his own, and that was all he cared about.

"Osbourne is at the hotel. You'll pick him up at two am and escort him to this address." Bás handed him a slip of paper with an address on it. "I'll be in place with the other parties."

"We expecting any trouble?"

"We always expect trouble but no more than usual if that's what you're asking me."

The car drew to a stop, and he and Bás stepped out and headed inside and straight for the elevator. Osbourne wanted to see him before the exchange, probably to issue a few more threats. Gunner had taken their beating to prove himself, but that didn't mean Osbourne trusted him.

He felt his lip curl in disgust. The man was only out for himself, putting his own men inside the Palace as personal protection was perfectly legal but knowing what he did, Gunner had serious concerns about the safety of the Royal Family but who could he tell? Jack and Eidolon knew the score already, and without any proof, they couldn't move in and take over without bringing the Palace in on this. With unknowns still at play, Jack would never show his hand.

He got off the elevator on the sixth-floor of the Imperial hotel and saw two men, obviously armed, standing outside the door to the only suite on this floor. They were wearing black suit jackets that only just hid the weapons they were carrying. As he approached, the larger man who he knew mostly spoke Latvian, stepped forward with a wand to make sure Gunner wasn't recording. Next, he held out his hand and Gunner placed his weapon in the man's hand.

It was laughable to him that these men believed he needed a weapon to harm Osbourne. If he wanted the man dead, he only needed his hands to accomplish that. Lucky for him, Gunner needed him alive for now.

Now satisfied that he was 'safe', Gunner stepped through the open door and saw Osbourne sitting in an armchair, leg crossed as he read some documents. He glanced up as Gunner entered and slowly moved to stand, placing the papers on the small coffee table beside him.

Osbourne was ex-military and still had the rigid bearing of a soldier. His shoulders straight, head high, eyes missing nothing. It's what made him good at seeing threats and had allowed him to climb the ranks to where he was now. He was tall, over six feet with grey hair cut short and a bulky build that had most likely been muscle once upon a time. Now it was mainly blubber from too much beer and fine dining and not enough time in the gym.

"Mr Ramberg, thank you for coming. I trust you have fully recovered from your mishap a few weeks ago?"

Gunner tried not to snort with laughter. His mishap had been a beating that left him barely able to stand and with two broken ribs. All of it so Osbourne could ensure his loyalty to him and the cause.

"Fully recovered, sir."

Osbourne nodded and began to pace for a moment. "Good, we have a lot to get done tonight, and I need to ensure you're fighting fit."

Gunner knew how to play the passive soldier, but his understanding had been that he was merely there as protection for Osbourne.

"I thought I was your protection tonight, sir?"

"Yes, you are, but as soon as this meeting is over, I have a job for you."

Osbourne was watching him now, studying his reaction to whatever he said next. It was another test he had to pass. Now that they no longer had Milla to hold over him they were continually testing his loyalty. That they believed Eidolon had killed her and Gunner was out for revenge was a tentative play. Not because Gunner wouldn't want revenge but because everyone who knew anything about Eidolon struggled to believe they would kill an innocent.

The autopsy photos and death certificate that Will had managed to leak online had helped, but there was still that shred of doubt no matter how small, that meant he was constantly being tested.

"What is the job?" He stood with his hands at his sides in a relaxed posture, but everything in him wanted to kill Osbourne for the way he'd blown up Gunner's life.

He stepped forward and handed Gunner a flash drive. He took it, turning it over in his hands before his eyes moved back to the Deputy Commissioner in question.

"I need you to get me the plans for the Royal Tour next year with all of the security details."

"How am I supposed to do that?"

"I guess you need to convince Jack that you're sorry."

"And if I can't?"

Osbourne shrugged. "Then the pretty thing you spent the other night with is going to get hurt."

Gunner made to move, his instincts to defend Lacey and pound this fucker to the ground, warring with his rational mind. He stopped the motion before Osbourne noticed and took the second while he sat back in his chair like some fucking lord of the manor to compose his features.

"There is no need to involve her. I have more than enough reason to hate Eidolon after what they did to Milla."

"Exactly. Now, I have calls to make so I will see you later."

Gunner was dismissed and not a moment too soon because he was fighting every impulse in his body to shoot Osbourne and be done with this shit. Only his desire to make right the wrongs he'd done helped him to bring his temper under control.

After collecting his gun from the guards at the door, he went back to the room he was sharing with Bás to wait for tonight. If the Irishman noticed his silence, he didn't say, and Gunner wasn't about to offer anything up voluntarily.

Around one-fifty-five they escorted Osbourne to his car with Bás riding in the front and Gunner beside the man in the bulletproof limo. His training had kicked in, and he was focused on tonight, having decided the only way to get past this next plan Osbourne had for him was to be straight with Jack and Alex, and pray they helped him for Lacey's sake if not for his.

The location of the meeting was more of a barn than a warehouse. The surrounding farmland giving it a desolate feel, especially at night with the damage from the recent storm evident for everyone to see. It was the perfect place to meet. Out of the way, remote, with excellent access and sightlines. Whoever had picked this place was a strategist with military training he was sure.

"Who picked this location?"

Osbourne cocked his head as he glanced out of the window at the dark shadows of the landscape. "My partner did. Why?"

"It's the perfect place for them to have an advantage."

"You best be on your game then, hadn't you?"

Gunner grunted something unintelligible and exited the car. He could feel eyes on him the second he did, the tingling in his neck a warning that he had multiple people watching him, most probably through the scope of a sniper rifle. Bás caught his eye, and he knew he felt it too. Gunner and Bás flanked Osbourne as he stepped from the car, and they ushered him quickly toward the barn where he could see soft light coming from under the door.

As they made it and the door opened, he let Bás move in first, with Gunner covering Osbourne's back. The room was set up with portable floodlights similar to those used for a photo shoot with eight guards standing in a semi-circle behind a man-child of Arabic ethnicity who was obviously Samir al-Sadir. To his left in a bespoke three-piece suit, sat Fredrick Granger—Jack and Will's scumbag of a father—and the truth Gunner had been trying to keep from them was finally glaring him in the face.

Chapter 6

Lacey stretched and rolled over in bed, taking in the sunlight coming in through her bedroom window. She could tell it was early, the August morning bright and full of hope, and she wanted desperately to share that hope. A new day full of promise and excitement, and it was all of those things but she couldn't get rid of the melancholy at waking up alone in her hotel room three days ago had brought her.

She'd looked for Gunner but hadn't been able to find him, his clothes and belongings already gone when she woke. The hotel wouldn't tell her if he'd checked into another room so she'd had to reluctantly accept that he was gone and would call her—or not.

Nate had picked her up at the airport. He, Skye, and some of the other guys from Fortis and Eidolon had very kindly helped her move her stuff into her new home. She'd barely had a second alone since she'd arrived. Lacey swung her legs out of bed, and throwing on a cream silk dressing gown, she went downstairs to her beautiful new kitchen to make herself a coffee.

Flicking the switch, she made herself some fruit and yoghurt, and taking her coffee went back upstairs to eat it on the balcony off her bedroom. Sitting on the rattan chair, she cupped the frothy latte and took her first sip of the sweet heaven that would bring the rest of her tired brain awake as she looked over at the view which had made her fall in love with this house.

The river Wye meandering in all its beauty was the most peaceful thing she could remember, and the body of water instantly made her think of Gunner and what he'd told her about his sister. It was hard not to let her heart break for the man who blamed himself for something which wasn't his fault.

The love he had for his sister was so pure, and she hated that he couldn't see himself how she saw him. Her body still ached in places from the things they'd done, and it made her want more. More of the bone tingling orgasms he could give her but not just that, although God knew the man was magnificent.

It was the way that despite his size and training, he never made her feel weak or scared or less. Not like Carmine had done—always telling her she was pathetic, throwing mock punches just to see her flinch and then laughing and putting his arms around her like it was all a big joke, but she knew it wasn't. The occasional slaps when they had a falling out had turned to hits and hair-pulling. Never enough to mark her body, because that was his cash cow—her modelling career his ticket to the lavish lifestyle and the prestige he thought he deserved.

As the youngest in the Russo crime family, Carmine had been treated as the family idiot by his father and older brothers. He'd allowed their treatment of him to make him into a bully. It had taken her a while to see it, but by then she'd felt trapped, weak like it was her fault he behaved the way he had.

She could ignore the affairs he had, the call girls and the waitresses. If it meant he left her alone she was glad for it, but when he began to pursue the models she worked with, she knew it was time to get out while she still had the tiniest bit of strength. It had been what happened with Skye and Noah that had been the final straw. Carmine had hidden her passport to stop her flying home to support her friend when she needed her, and that was when she'd left him.

Carmine had thought it all a game at first, but when he realised she meant it, he'd begun to send her gifts and turn up at her shoots until she'd known she had to leave and make a fresh start. She never expected it to be her friend's wedding where she'd make a clean break and in such a fashion.

The scars from that still had the power to break her if she let them but with therapy and support from good friends like Skye, Lizzie, and surprisingly Roz, she'd managed to get her life back on track.

Deciding to move here to this tranquil piece of England and work with Callie Lund, another model and who was now engaged to Reid, one of the guys who had saved her that day, had felt right—good.

Her phone rang on her nightstand, where it was charging, and she moved to answer it, wondering who it was at this time of the morning—barely seven am.

Lacey smiled as she saw the name on the ID said 'Skye' and answered.

"Morning, sweetie. Hope I didn't wake you, but I wanted to catch you before you got busy in the office and forgot the outside world existed."

Lacey couldn't deny that when she started to design her kids and teens range she got utterly lost in it.

"Actually, I have a meeting with Callie and Taamira today to go over the range for next summer. I want their take on it."

"Oh, good. That makes my life easier."

Lacey could hear Nancy in the background and knew Skye was probably feeding the kids breakfast while she talked. The sound of Nate's deep voice close to the phone, calling hello, and then kissing his wife before heading out made her smile for her friend. Skye deserved every second of happiness she got, and anyone could see that man loved her to bits.

Ignoring the little bite of longing, she concentrated on what Skye had said instead. "Life easier how?"

"Girls night tonight, all of us are going. It's time to leave the kids with their dads and head out on the town. Can you invite Callie, and Taamira? I'll get Roz to ask Evelyn, Pax, and the others. I already asked Autumn, and she's up for it too."

Lacey was about to try and wriggle out of it but then realised a girl's night was exactly what she needed. "Fine, I'll speak to them. What's the plan?"

"Why don't you come here and get ready with me like we used to, minus the Lambrini and grape 20/20." Skye gave a mock shudder over the phone, which made Lacey smile.

"Sounds good. What time?"

"Come over around six, and we can get some food in before we get ready. I'm way too old for drinking on an empty stomach. Eating is definitely not cheating."

Lacey laughed, and a few minutes later they hung up. Lacey was still smiling as she walked back out onto the balcony and froze as she saw a man standing at the tree line to her property that led toward the river. Stepping back, she reached for her phone, and when she spun around, he was gone.

She looked for any sign of someone hanging around but found nothing and then felt silly. The break-in at the hotel had been a disgruntled hotel employee, and hers hadn't been the only room trashed. She'd been grateful when the hotel manager called to tell her and decided against filing charges, just wanting a quiet life but now she saw threats where there was only sunshine, and she cursed her paranoia.

With a shake of her head, she brushed the silliness away and went to get ready for her day, a spring in her step at the thought of girl's night with her new friends. It was Friday night, she had plans for the first time in ages, and it felt good. The only thing she had to do was to get through tonight without drinking or arousing her friend's suspicions about it. Explaining her one-night stand with Gunner wasn't something she was ready for just yet.

Eight hours later, Lacey realised that not spilling her guts to her friends was going to be more challenging than she thought. They had eaten dinner of homemade fajitas, and she'd met Autumn who was every bit as lovely as Skye had said she was. Mitch had walked her over to Nate and Skye's home, which was just a few doors away despite her telling him it wasn't necessary.

Skye grinned as Mitch backed away with Maggie, Autumns baby daughter in his arms and waved at Autumn. "That man is head over heels for you."

"I know," Autumn sighed, and Lacey laughed.

"I don't think he's the only one head over heels."

Autumn blushed but didn't deny it.

They had gotten ready to the sound of Nate bathing Nancy, and Noah calling out his times tables from the bedroom as Nate quizzed him. It was chaos and beautiful, and Lacey would give her right arm for a life like this. She continued applying her mascara as she considered how she would feel if she was carrying Gunner's baby and found that while it wasn't the ideal situation, she wouldn't regret it or see it as a bad thing. If she was honest with herself and she always tried to be these days, she wanted to be pregnant.

As it was still light, the three women had decided to walk into town. The bar where they were meeting the others wasn't far away. Nate had insisted they get a cab, but Skye had told him he was ridiculous and had seemingly won that battle, but as Waggs stepped out from his front door where he rented a room from Mitch, it became apparent that Skye hadn't won, Nate had just beaten a tactical retreat.

"Evening, ladies, out for a stroll?"

40

Autumn cocked her eyebrow at the blond-haired man who was Eidolon's field medic and had looked after Lacey after her kidnapping. He gave her a chin lift hello, and she remembered how safe he'd made her feel as he treated her. A gentle warrior with an air of calm he'd made her feel less afraid.

"Waggs, I see you got the short straw of walking us into town."

Waggs held up his hands in surrender. "Just taking a walk."

He fell into step beside them, and Skye took out her phone and texted someone.

"Nate is acting all innocent."

Autumn shrugged. "They care. It's hard to be mad at that."

"I guess."

They got to the door of the Gin bar and stopped, and Lacey glanced at Waggs. "Thank you for escorting us, but I think we have it from here, unless you want to join girl's night for a dance?"

Waggs, the scary military-trained Special Forces soldier, practically blanched at her invitation.

"No thanks, I'm good." With that he was gone, and giggling, she and the others were swallowed into the bar.

Lacey had never accepted so many hugs in her life. Evelyn, who was married to Alex, who'd been the fake priest when Carmine kidnapped her and demanded she marry him. Pax who was engaged to Blake, Callie and Taamira, who she knew really well and now partnered with. They were also dating Reid and Liam, respectively. A heavily pregnant Roz sat next to Astrid, who was stunning and could've easily been a model herself. Skye was talking to Ava, Lauren, and Lucy about a first birthday cake for Lucy's daughter. Aubrey and Mara were out on the dance floor with Bebe, and Lacey was just taking it all in.

"Ladies, the gentlemen over there just sent these over." A waitress set a tray full of shots on the table and Lacey looked around to where she'd indicated and laughed as she saw what could only be described as a horde of Special Forces husbands and partners watching the women they loved.

"How did they get out?" Lauren asked as she took the shot and knocked it back.

"The in-laws, I bet," Skye said, knocking back her shot with a shake of her head.

41

Lizzie leaned in close. "Don't worry, they won't crash the party until we give them the green light. They know they get no monkey sex otherwise."

Lacey giggled at the image of these men chomping at the bit to get to their women but holding back because they didn't want to unleash their wrath.

"Ha. like I can do monkey sex in my state," Roz grumbled.

"Quit whining, Roz. Everyone knows you love being pregnant."

Roz just glared at Astrid. "I think I have a new assignment for you in Antarctica."

"You wouldn't."

"Oh, we both know I would."

"Roz, did you get the girls to look at the designs I sent you?"

Roz beamed and started telling Lacey what her girls Natalia and Katarina had thought about the designs, and Astrid mouthed her thanks to her.

"Hey, Lacey, your shot." Skye lifted the glass to her, and Lacey froze, panic setting in as her friends watched her expectantly.

"No, I don't fancy it."

"Oh, come on, Lacey."

"Forget it. She's been dumping her drinks all night." Bebe walked up behind her and Lacey turned to glare at the woman.

Skye frowned, closing one eye and crossed her arms. "Spill it."

"I'm just not drinking at the moment."

"Why?"

Lacey crossed and uncrossed her legs the sequin mini skirt riding up her toned thighs. "Do I need a reason?"

"No, but you have one. Are you pregnant?"

"No, yes, maybe?"

The table erupted in squeals which had a few of the men—Zack and Alex if she wasn't mistaken—moving toward them only to stop when Evelyn shook her head. She'd have laughed if her best friend didn't have her pinned with a no-bullshit look.

"Well, which is it?"

Lacey sighed, wishing she was better at this kind of stuff. Every woman at the table was staring now waiting for the gossip they knew was coming. "I might be, but I don't know yet."

"How did this happen?"

Lacey shrugged. "The usual way. I had sex and forgot to use protection."

"Wow, was it wild, blow your head amazing sex?" Astrid asked, leaning in close.

"Yes." Lacey couldn't eradicate the memory of her night with Gunner and now allowing herself to relive it, she realised it had been all that and more.

"Do we know him?" Skye had finally put the shot back on the table.

Lacey wasn't sure what to do now. She didn't want to lie, but she had a feeling something had happened with Gunner and Eidolon that was bad, and half these women were married or engaged to Eidolon operatives. Would they give her the answers she found herself needing, or would they confuse her more? Knowing the only answers that would plague her were the ones she didn't know, she decided to be honest. "Yes. It was Gunner."

"Eidolon's Gunner?" Pax said slowly as she placed her drink on the table.

Lacey looked across at Pax who had glance across at her fiancé Blake.

"Yes."

"Oh, girl. What did you do?" Skye asked sadly.

Lacey realised as the table went deafeningly silent that she'd just made   a   huge   mistake.

Chapter 7

He'd known the second he set foot in Hereford that he had eyes on him, and they weren't Eidolon. That wasn't unexpected, and the men watching him were low-level punks meant to, in Bás' words, keep him on track. If they were trying to scare him, then Osbourne honestly had no idea who Gunner was or that he had fuck all left to lose.

Except he did now—maybe he did now, and that was how he found himself standing in the forest at the back of Lacey's new home looking up at the dark house that overlooked the river. He'd been around this part of town before and liked it a lot, although it was way out of his budget with all the fees he paid for Milla, and honestly, a house was just a place to sleep for him, so he didn't need fancy rooms or big gardens.

But none of that was on his mind right now. His main concern centred around the two men watching Lacey's house. These weren't like the thugs watching him; no, these two had training. Unlucky for them, he'd had more training and tactical awareness. That was another thing to come from Eidolon. It wasn't enough to be the best sniper or an explosives expert; you had to be the best at all of it.

Jack made sure they could survive in a jungle, in the mountains in the dead of winter, and every other condition known to man, because they'd never known where their missions or work for the Royal Family would take them. They needed to be ready for the ugliest humanity had to offer.

Gunner had a choice to make, but before he got the chance to make it, he saw headlights pull into Lacey's drive and the excitement at seeing her again made his body feel energised. Moving closer but keeping aware of the men watching her, he frowned when he saw Waggs get out of the car and walk Lacey to her door.

Jealousy slithered through him, and he had the sudden urge to punch his teammate in the face. He had no right. Lacey didn't belong to him, most likely never would, but it didn't stop his feet moving toward the front door when he saw Waggs follow her inside and close the door.

44

He watched from the shadows, doubt slithering through him as he waited to see if his former friend would leave quickly. But as the minutes ticked on and he didn't, Gunner could feel the anger begin to course through his blood. Breaking cover, he walked up to the door and was surprised when it opened, and he saw Waggs standing there with his arms crossed baring his way.

Waggs had always been the quiet one, the calm one under pressure. He and Gunner had gotten on well, but as Waggs glared at him now, he knew the resentment at what he'd done still ran deep, and he didn't blame him. But this wasn't about that; this was about the woman who was standing behind Waggs looking nervous.

"Decided to stop hiding, Gunner?"

"Why are you here, Waggs?"

Waggs glanced back at Lacey with a grin and tipped his head. "What's it to you?"

Gunner clenched his fists and then forced calm into his voice. "Can we do this inside?"

Once again Waggs glanced at Lacey who nodded, filling him with relief. He had no idea what they'd told her about him and in truth, he had no defence. Whatever they said he'd done was true, and if she wanted nothing to do with him, he wouldn't blame her. But he wouldn't abandon her or his child if there was one, no matter how much she hated him.

Waggs stepped back from the door and allowed him to walk past before he closed the door and followed both him and Lacey inside. The house was perfectly Lacey, open airy and yet warm and inviting. He knew she'd only just moved in and yet he could already see flashes of her personality here and there.

It was a home, not just a house, and he felt it was in no small part to the woman who was looking at him with wariness in her eyes. He drank in the short silver sequin skirt that hugged her creamy thighs and the black camisole top that showed just the hint of cleavage. She was stunning and classy and way too good for him, but he couldn't remember wanting someone the way he wanted her.

Not just in a physical way, although God knew she brought him to his knees with wanting her but being close to her and hearing about her day. Eating dinner with her or even just watching tv together while she was in his arms.

"Can we talk, Cosmo?"

Lacey looked wary, and he could see the hurt on her face at the way he'd left in Germany. He never explained himself, but he felt the need deep inside him to right the wrong he'd done to her.

"I can stay if you need me to, Lacey?" Waggs crossed his arms as he moved closer to the woman who was fast coming to mean everything to Gunner.

"What the fuck is your problem, Waggs? I get that you hate my guts but don't ever think for one second that Lacey is in any danger from me. I would rather rip out my own heart than hurt a hair on her head."

He saw Lacey's eyes widen in surprise at his outburst, but his concentration was firmly on Waggs.

"Is that what you think? That I hate you? I don't hate you, Gunner. I just don't trust you."

Gunner took that blow even though it hurt like hell because he deserved it. "I get that, but I promise you on Milla's life, I won't hurt this woman."

Waggs stared at him for a moment, not giving anything away before he looked at Lacey.

"It's fine. Thanks for seeing me home and checking the house for me. I don't know why it spooked me."

"No problem, Lacey. A friend of Skye's is a friend of mine. That woman can bake."

Lacey sputtered out a laugh. "That she can."

Gunner stayed put while Lacey walked Waggs to the door and let him out, locking up behind him. When she turned, she had her arms crossed over her midriff in a protective gesture which he hated. Everything in him wanted to go to her and pull her against him but did he even have the right after he'd left? More than that, should he pull her closer into his orbit when it would likely put her in more danger?

His mind went to the men outside in the woods, and he figured it was already too late. She was already in danger, certainly from the people he was forced to work with but maybe others too and he needed to find out who they were, but first he needed to wipe that look of despair off her face.

"Come here, Lacey."

He'd thought she'd refuse, but she made a tentative step towards him, and he moved the rest of the way, opening his arms up to her and feeling ten feet tall when she moved into his embrace.

Her scent surrounded him, wiping out all the doubt that had slithered through his mind like an ugly serpent. As her arms came around him and she settled against him, everything seemed right with the world. He wanted to stand there and bask in the moment, freeze time so they could stay this way and not face the questions and recriminations he knew would come when she found out what he'd done.

He felt her shiver against his chest and rubbed her arms with his hands before kissing her head. "Let's sit down for a minute."

Lacey seemed fortified as he let her go and instantly hated the distance between them. Everything in him wanted to take her to bed and reaffirm the connection they'd shared in Germany, but he was loathe to push her into anything further without the facts.

"Would you like a drink? Tea, coffee?"

Gunner shook his head. "No, thanks." He followed her into the kitchen where she poured herself a glass of water and then sat at the island facing the back of the house. He thought about the men watching her home and was glad she'd closed the blinds.

Sitting on the stool beside her, he turned her to face him, capturing her legs between his knees.

"I owe you an explanation."

Lacey shook her head. "You don't owe me anything, Gunner."

He blew out a frustrated breath. "Okay, I want to explain."

"I was out with my friends tonight and when I wasn't drinking, Skye pinned me with her 'mum' look and demanded to know why."

Gunner took her wrist in his hand and rubbed the pulse point gently, just needing to touch her in some way. "Did you tell her?"

"Yes, and then she and all the girls wanted to know whose it was and when I said your name, it was like I had dropped a bomb on the place. Everyone looked at me with pity, and I had to get out of there. I was walking home when Waggs pulled up. Skye had called Nate, who called Waggs and he gave me a lift. When I got here, I got spooked, and he offered to check out the house for me."

Gunner pulled back at her admission, running his hand through his hair in frustration. He hated that everyone's reaction to him had blindsided her. He looked away before making eye contact with the woman who was giving him a reason to live, and not because she might be pregnant but because he suddenly had the urge to want a life again. For the first time in more years than he could remember, he wanted more.

"You know about Milla, but what you don't know is about two years ago some people kidnapped her." He heard her indrawn breath and saw the compassion on her face, feeling her fingers on his thigh made him continue past the lump in his throat.

"A man I didn't know knocked on my door and said they had my sister, and if I wanted her to stay alive, I would do as they asked."

"What did they want from you?"

"To sabotage Eidolon, to feed them information that would weaken the team. They said if I didn't, they would kill her, but first, they would rape her. I wanted to kill him, still do but I had no choice. If I told Jack or the others, they said they would know. I had to wear a wire at all times, and if I took it off, they would hurt her."

"You did what any brother would do, Gunner. You protected your sister. She was weaker than Eidolon. They could protect themselves, but she only had you."

"You don't understand. I betrayed my friends, the men who'd had my back." He stood and began to pace as his shame leaked out between them like a pool of tar.

Lacey stayed him with her hand. "You did what you had to do. My guess is none of them blames you for that. Any brother would've done the same thing. They're probably butt hurt and feeling slighted."

Gunner smirked when he would never have believed humour possible in this situation. "I'm not sure butt hurt is something I would use to describe their reaction."

"Where is Milla now?"

"Jack and the boys rescued her with Fortis but made it look like they killed her. Now the people who were blackmailing me think I'm working for them because I hate Eidolon."

"But in reality, you're working both sides of this, aren't you? Trying to please everyone and keep everything together and nobody has your back."

"I don't deserve what they're giving me, and that's a chance to redeem myself."

"Bullshit. You made a mistake, probably some bad ones but you did it for the right reasons, and you're trying to make it right." Lacey paced, her arms crossed, looking fucking beautiful. "Tell me something, if Jack or Waggs had done the same, how would you feel?"

Gunner shrugged. "What does it matter?"

"Humour me."

"I don't know, disappointed."

"Would you turn your back on them?"

"No, never."

"Exactly, but they've done nothing to help you out, only judged and hung you out to dry."

"It isn't as simple as that, Lacey." He couldn't explain about the other secret he'd kept from Jack and Will, knowing he needed to tell them first, which was another reason he was here.

"Maybe not, but it isn't all your fault either."

Gunner remained silent, not ready to go there yet. "Either way, I should've warned you after what we did in Germany and knowing you were coming here."

"It's fine. I didn't get the feeling they were angry with you, just sad."

"I have more to tell you but not tonight. I didn't come here to seek forgiveness for my sins."

"Why did you come?"

Gunner moved closer, his hand brushing her hip. "Because I can't stay away from you."

"Good because I want you here. Whatever happens with Jack and Eidolon, I know down to my soul that you're a good man, Gunner. You may have lost sight of that, but I know it."

Gunner cupped her nape, running his thumb over her full lips. "You make me want things I shouldn't."

"Like?"

"A   future,   Lacey."

Chapter 8

Lacey didn't know how to respond to Gunner's comment about not being able to stay away from her, so she kept quiet.

"Have you got somewhere to stay tonight?" Her question must have surprised him because he took a step back and she wondered if he thought she was trying to get rid of him. She wasn't. The truth was she liked him in her home. The feeling of safety she felt around him was only surpassed by the desire that flooded her veins when he was near.

"I can find somewhere. Don't worry about me, Cosmo." He put some distance between them.

"You can stay here. The truth is, I've been feeling spooked the last few days."

Gunner spun back to her, closing the gap instantly, a look of awareness in his blue eyes as he surveyed the room.

"Did something happen?"

Lacey wrinkled her nose. "Not really, I thought I saw someone in the woods behind the house, but I realise it's probably my overactive imagination."

Gunner opened his mouth and then closed as if thinking better of what he'd been about to say. He closed the gap between them, tilting her head up with his finger and she sucked in a breath at the heat she saw in his eyes. "If I stay here, I'll want to be in your bed, and if I'm in your bed, I'll want to be inside you."

Lacey swallowed, giving herself more time to make a decision. The truth was the desire in her belly, the heat pooling between her leg, as she imagined him touching her. Lacey licked her lips that were suddenly dry, and Gunner groaned, making her look up into his liquid eyes.

"I'm okay with all of those things."

"Jesus fucking Christ."

With one movement she was in his arms, and he was kissing her as if he hadn't seen her in months and she was the fuel he needed to live. It was consuming and perfect, the scent of his shower gel and something that was entirely Gunner surrounded her adding to the need building inside her.

She didn't care that others thought he was bad news; all she cared about was what was between them. A connection that had begun years ago and had flared in Germany. Maybe it was fate bringing them together, and perhaps it was a coincidence, she didn't know or care. All she knew was that when something felt this good, it would be foolish to ignore it.

Gunner pulled away and was breathing fast as he moved toward the living space.

"I can't think when I'm around you, Lacey. You consume me."

It was a frank admission from a man she thought probably kept most things close to his chest.

"Is that a problem?"

Gunner smirked as she moved closer to him, his eyes roving over her, making her feel more beautiful than all the photographers in the world ever had.

"Yeah, Cosmo, it is in some ways. I'm a man with a lot of enemies, and dragging you into my world as I have, put a target on you. To keep you safe, I have to keep my head."

Lacey didn't want to consider the danger he was talking about, at least not tonight.

"How about in here, in this house, you let me quiet the thoughts that plague you?" She was standing in front of him now and lifted her hand to run a finger down his temple. Watching as his eyes closed. "But out there, you're who you need to be to keep us safe."

"How can you trust me after everything I told you?"

His voice was rough like broken glass as he asked the question, and she knew that no matter how hard others had been on him in the past he'd been harder—blaming himself for things that weren't his to carry. She had the overwhelming need to protect this man, to heal him.

Not because she thought this had broken him but because he was hurting badly, and nobody could see except her, and that made her angry. He was a good man who'd done some bad things. She knew enough to know he'd varnished over things through shame, but a man who could treat her with such gentleness and love his sister as he did wasn't who he thought himself to be.

"How can I not? I see a good man who has made some wrong turns and taken the blame when it wasn't his to carry. You've only ever treated me with compassion and tenderness, and that is why I trust you."

Gunner cupped her face in his hands. "You make me want to be that man you describe."

"You are already, but I see it might take some time, which is fine. Will you be sticking around Hereford for a while?"

Gunner nodded. "Yes, I have some business with Eidolon to deal with."

He wanted to say more she could feel it, but he didn't. Instead, he kissed her nose. "Why don't you go on up and I'll set the alarm and make sure the house is secure?"

Lacey nodded and turned for the stairs.

"Lacey?"

She turned on the first step. "Yes?"

"If you want me on the couch, that's fine. I don't want to push you into anything you're not ready for or don't want. I already did that once."

"First, I don't offer my bed to any man, so take it as read that I want you there, and second, you didn't push me into anything. If I remember rightly, I was the one who made the first move and jumped your bones when you were vulnerable. So, if there's any blame, it's mine."

Gunner snorted. "You can jump me any time, Cosmo."

Lacey smiled at the confident man self-assuredness he showed in that comment.

"See you upstairs."

Lacey turned and walked upstairs a smile curving her lips. She walked into her bedroom and stopped dead. Fear like a block of ice running up her spine as she saw the familiar nightwear laid out on the bed. Her vision began to tunnel, her body frozen as if paralysed, sweat beading on her chest.

The same nightwear Carmine Russo had made her wear was laid out exactly as he'd done every night. Except this time there was a bloody knife lying in the middle of it. The sight of the blood on the white, silk nightgown snapped her out of her fog, and she let out a terrified scream. Every memory of the things Carmine had done to her coming at her like blows, each one was cutting her deeper and making her feel weaker and more afraid than the last.

Moments later, she felt strong arms come around her, and Gunner turned her into his chest.

"It's okay, Lacey. I have you."

Lacey burrowed closer, wanting to absorb the safety of his arms around her. She let Gunner guide her from the room and back down the stairs and sit her on the couch as he pulled a blanket from the back over her shoulders. Lacey didn't realise it until then, but she was shivering so hard she was shaking.

Gunner sat beside her, one arm holding on to her, the other using his phone. It was hard to focus on the now; all she could feel was fear and terror that she was being pulled back into the hell she thought she'd escaped.

She'd thought moving here would give her the safety and home she craved, but now it was being tainted by her past, one she thought she could escape.

"Waggs, it's Gunner. I need you to come to Lacey's place now and bring a few of the team, please. We have a situation."

Lacey felt Gunner place the phone down and wrapped his other arm around her, and that was when she noticed he had his gun drawn by his side. She knew he would protect her and the comfort it offered eased her fears just enough that she stopped shaking, but she didn't pull away from Gunner's arms, and he didn't ease his hold in the least.

"I should have known he'd never give me up." Her words sounded hollow even to her own ears.

"I won't let him or any of his people hurt you, Lacey."

"He already did."

Gunner kissed her head and held on tight as if he could keep her together with just his will alone. Lacey knew that if anyone could, it would be him.

"I know he did, Cosmo, and I'm so sorry he hurt you, but I promise you he won't hurt you again. On my life, I'll protect you and give you a chance at the life you want."

"Thank you, Gunner."

"Anything for you, Lacey. You've given me more reason to live in the last four days than I have had my entire adult life. There is nothing I won't do for you."

Lacey believed him, and that spoke volumes about the man who was edging his way deeper into her heart with every word and action.

"Why, Ramberg?"

Gunner started, and she looked up as he pulled slightly away. "What?"

"Well, you're Ramberg, but your sister is Eivinsdóttir."

"Oh, that. No mystery really. I was born Gunner Eivinsson. As the male in the family, the name has 'son' at the end and a daughter will have 'dottir'. My father's name was Eivin and then either son or dottir depending on if it's a boy or girl. The reason I went by Ramberg was that I wanted to protect my sister and grandmother from my job and keep that part of my life private. So, I changed it when I joined the forces, and now it's more a part of me than my original name."

"It's very complex."

Gunner shrugged. "I guess it is if you don't grow up with it as I did."

Lacey liked talking to Gunner. He was intelligent and interesting and made her feel calm when she'd been about to have a meltdown. His presence in her life was unexpected to say the least, but it was so very welcome, and she hoped it continued because she wasn't ready to say goodbye to this man and had the frightening feeling she may never want to.

Chapter 9

Gunner walked into the building that housed the Eidolon operation and felt a familiar melancholy assail him. This place, the buildings, the fitness course outside the kitchen where Alex cooked, held such good memories for him. He'd spent the best days of his life in this place, and the thought that he was only here as a guest now damn near broke him.

Last night it had been instinctual to call Waggs and ask for his help, but when the entire Eidolon team showed up, he'd been shocked. He shouldn't have. These men were a team, and they played together and worked together, and when one was in trouble, they all came running.

He knew they had only come because it was Lacey and she was close to Nate and Skye, but it had still felt good for just a minute. His proudest moments had been serving with these men, working to rid the world of evil and protect the monarchy.

Alex had brought Evelyn, his partner who was as deadly as any of the men, and she'd sat with Lacey while she explained what she'd found. He'd then explained what he'd seen in the woods. It had been agreed that he would stay overnight with Lacey and he'd seen a few raised eyebrows but ignored it.

Alex and Blake had also stayed to keep watch from outside. Now he was here so he could tell the team about what he knew, but he owed it to Jack to tell him and Will first. It was something he'd desperately hoped to avoid, but the time had come where he could no longer deny the truth.

He paused at the door to the gym, seeing the sparring ring in the middle where he'd kicked ass and had his ass kicked so many times and then followed it up with a drink down the pub.

"Been a while since we got in the ring together."

Gunner glanced sideways at Waggs, noting his words held no anger just cold hard facts. "Yeah, it has."

"Do you regret it?"

Gunner didn't have to ask what he was talking about, they had been close once, as close as brothers before he blew it all up.

"Every day and yet every day, I don't see how I could have made a different choice. You saw Milla, she was so vulnerable, and I'd already taken enough from her."

Waggs nodded, staying silent as if absorbing what Gunner had admitted. It was hard to tell people you had hurt and betrayed that you would do it again, but Gunner had lied enough, and he owed these men nothing but the truth now.

"I never saw it before, but I see it now."

Gunner cocked his head as he faced Waggs who was studying him intently.

"Saw what?"

"You blame yourself for her being the way she is."

Gunner snorted and looked away. "Good reason for that, I fucking am."

"Tell me something. If this was the other way around and Milla was healthy, and you were in her place, would you want her to blame herself as you do?"

"Of course not, but regardless of that, I still betrayed this team."

"Yes, you did."

Gunner hadn't expected Waggs' agreement to hurt so much.

"But I can't say in all honesty I wouldn't have done the same thing in your place. If I could go back and save my twin, I don't think there would be any price I wasn't willing to pay. And if anyone says different, I think they're lying."

Gunner felt the emotion like a punch to the gut. He knew Waggs grieved the loss of his twin but didn't know the full story and had never asked, preferring to let the man keep his secrets so he could keep his.

Waggs held out his hand and Gunner looked at it for a moment not sure if he was reading things correctly, but Waggs kept it there until Gunner shook it.

"I'm sorry I wasn't there when you needed me, and I'm sorry I never gave you the benefit of the doubt. I know the man you are, and I should've looked for a reason instead of acting all hurt and betrayed. I let you down, and I regret it. But for what it's worth, I have your back now and if you need anything, just ask." With that, Waggs walked away, leaving Gunner feeling shocked to his core.

"Ready to get this meeting started?"

Gunner hadn't heard him come up behind him. Jack was like a panther unseen, silent, deadly. He in no way wanted to have this conversation, but it was time, so he nodded his head.

He followed Jack back to his pristine office that had the Monarch's seal in a frame on the wall. It was uncluttered and organised like the man himself. Gunner nodded at Will, who was the polar opposite of Jack—covered in tattoos, a wild child who skirted the rules to achieve what he needed, even had a short stint in juvey which had caused a rift between the brothers for a long time.

"Gunner."

"Will."

Jack rounded his desk and sat and offered Gunner a seat, which he took, tilting it at an angle so he could see the door.

"How is Lacey this morning?" Jack asked as he sat back in his chair and rested his hands across his flat abdomen. He looked relaxed, calm, but anyone that knew him could see he was far from it. He was assessing every move Gunner made, looking for a lie or a weakness, something that would threaten him or those he cared about.

"She seems fine."

"I hear you met her in Germany?"

Gunner stayed silent wondering if Lacey had told the girls and it got back to Jack or if someone else had been watching.

"Enough chit chat. I have information, and I feel you and Will need to hear it first."

"Go on."

"Osbourne took me to meet his partner, who had set up the meeting with Samir al-Sadir."

"And that man was my father."

Gunner reared back in surprise at Will's statement.

"Yes, how did you know?"

Will laughed without humour and looked at Jack, whose jaw was working overtime as he ground his teeth and tried to hold his temper. There had only been a few times that Gunner could remember seeing Jack lose his legendary cool, but if he wasn't mistaken, he was very close to it now.

"Our father is the reason I went to jail. He was working with Miqdaad al-Sadir, and when I caught him, he engineered it so I ended up in prison. He promised he'd cut ties and Jack ensured that was the case when he formed Eidolon and took him out."

"Yes, I remember that mission."

"So, my father is working with Osbourne and Samir now but to what end?" Jack pursed his lips, having got his anger under control.

"I don't know, but Osbourne is out for your blood, and Fredrick knows it."

"He has never had much use for his sons. I was always a disappointment to him, and Jack was his hero until he couldn't control him anymore. Now we're both expendable. The only reason he's still alive is because of our mother."

"Did you know he was working with Osbourne?"

Jack shook his head. "No not until you mentioned Miqdaad. Which begs the question, did you know my father was involved in all this?"

Gunner sucked in a large breath before letting it out slowly. "I suspected from the start but couldn't be sure. The man who came to my door and blackmailed me about Milla was only the messenger, but I caught sight of the man in the back of the car when he left, and I thought I recognised him as your father but wasn't one hundred per cent. I wasn't willing to blow your life up if I wasn't sure."

"So, my father targeted you from the start. He was the one to blow this team up."

Gunner shook his head. "Not only him, Jack. I should have come to you."

"Yeah, how?"

Gunner stood and began to pace. "I don't know."

"Exactly. If there had been another way you would have found it. We see that now, Gunner, we all do."

"But I betrayed you all, Jesus I let them hurt Pax."

"I know, and while that is far from ideal, we know you wouldn't have let that happen if there had been any way to avoid it. Blake hates it, but he does understand it."

"You shouldn't trust me. I let people down."

"Tough shit, because you're part of this team and we should have had your back before, and we didn't, and for that, I'm truly sorry. But we have it now, and we'll take my father down and make him pay for what he's done once and for all."

Gunner sank into the chair, shocked to say the very least at the turn of events today had taken. "I need to stay undercover. It's the only way to find out how far this goes."

Jack stood and came around the desk and leaned against it as Will took his seat and began to type on the laptop there.

"Agreed. What did they want you to do?"

"Osbourne wants the plans and itinerary for the Royal Tour next year."

"That's easy. We can mock that up and send him a fake."

Gunner shook his head. "No. If he has someone inside the Palace who has seen the originals he'll know we're on to him."

"So, we give him the plans. We can always change it afterwards. I can ask for an audience with Her Majesty and explain what's happening under the guise of something else. I think it's way past time to bring her in on this."

"What about her safety? You can't trust Osbourne."

"I have someone I can put in place undercover who can be with her at all times."

Gunner didn't ask, and Jack didn't offer any more information. "It can't look like I got this information easily. Osbourne told me to wheedle my way back in, and he knows you. Knows you won't fall for that easily."

"That's fine. Stay in Hereford and work the situation with Lacey and make it seem like you're making friends with the team by showing up here and being seen with a few of the guys out and about."

"What about Bás?"

Jack glanced at Will, who gave the slightest nod of his head. "Let us handle Bás."

"Fine. Is there anything else I can do here?" Gunner was still far from sure about his position with Eidolon or his former teammates, but for the first time in two years, he didn't feel like an outsider.

"No, do what Osbourne asked and report back as he told you to. Tell him it's taking time. In the meantime, sort out the situation with Lacey and find out if her sicko ex is behind this latest threat."

"Oh, believe me, protecting Lacey is top of my list."

Jack cocked his head and groaned. "Not another one? My men are falling like flies. Is there some kind of vaccine I can get from this stupidity?"

Will punched his brother on the arm. "Dick don't knock it until you try it. Aubrey is the best thing to ever happen to me."

Jack swiped him back, causing Will to stumble and Gunner to laugh at the antics of these grown men, brothers as close as anyone could be.

"Well, that's true. If you and Aubrey ever split up, I want to keep her and get rid of you."

"Bro, there's no way Aubrey would leave me. She loves me."

"No accounting for taste hey, brother."

"Whatever. I have to go see Mum and talk about the wedding. I'm tempted to put it off with everything going on with Dad, but I'll speak to Aubrey first. I personally don't want that asshole in my wedding pictures."

"Don't tip your hand that you know. He needs to believe that Gunner hasn't told us and is keeping his cover."

"This isn't my first rodeo, Jack."

Will shook his head and lifted his hand as he left.

"You look a little shell-shocked, Gunner."

Gunner stroked his chin. "Honestly, I am. I never once considered you would forgive me or that I deserved it."

Jack motioned for the door, and he followed. "Honestly, neither did I, but I see now how we all made mistakes, and so do the rest of the team. If you can't forgive family, then there's not much hope for the world, and you are family, Gunner. I just hope you can forgive us. I don't say it will go back to how it was, but that doesn't mean we can't all grow from this and learn to be better men."

They stopped at the door to the gym, and he saw Mitch and Alex in the ring sparring. Mitch threw a left hook and Alex blocked and countered with a one-two punch and an arm lock until Mitch tapped out. The two men stopped as he and Jack entered, and Mitch walked to the side of the ropes slowly.

Mitch had reason to hate him. He'd tied him up so he could get away when Mitch had rumbled him as the traitor. Gunner waited for the inevitable hate and only just caught the gloves Jack threw him.

"Time to get back in the ring and see how much fitness you lost while you were on your sabbatical."

Alex barked out a laugh as Jack got his own gloves on and Gunner did the same. "Sabbatical? Is that what we're calling it?"

"Calling it a holiday seems a little unfair considering he got beaten up."

Gunner let the words flow around him, the banter one of the things he'd missed the most. Today hadn't gone as he'd expected, but it had gone infinitely better. And the one person he couldn't wait to share that with was Lacey. It should scare him how much he was falling for her, but for perhaps the first time in his life he didn't let the   fear   of   loving   someone   win.

Chapter 10

Nate had dropped Lacey off at her home leaving her with Liam and Reid, two of the Eidolon guys. Skye had held her while she cried and forced her to talk through her fears about Carmine, reassuring her at each turn that he wouldn't get near her.

Lacey loved Skye. She was her oldest friend, and there was nobody she'd trusted more until Gunner. He'd barrelled into her life like a bulldozer, turning it upside down in the best way. Now the only time she felt safe was when he was around. Of course, she'd never tell him that, she wouldn't want to put any more on him than she already had.

As she'd lain in his arms last night, she'd come to the conclusion he could be hanging around just to see if she was pregnant. When it turned out that she more than likely wasn't, he'd politely back away. It hurt her heart to think it, but why else would he stay? As Carmine had taken great pains to remind her, she was boring and cold in bed.

Although it had felt far from cold being with Gunner, the boring part was probably right. She'd done parties and premiers, and she had no desire to go out and get drunk every night. Staying home and reading a book or working on a design was how she liked to spend her time.

Poking her head in the fridge, she pondered what to make for dinner. Gunner was staying with her for now, and she wanted to embrace it and cherish every second while she had him. She was pulling peppers and a package of chicken breasts from the fridge when she heard the front door open.

Lacey knew it was him without hearing a single word, just the feeling and energy he brought into the room was enough, and she closed her eyes and sighed. Everything suddenly felt right with her world again. She hadn't realised the tension she was carrying until he was in her space and she felt it ebb away.

Gunner rounded the corner to the kitchen and Lacey dropped the ingredients onto the counter and hurried to him.

"Your face. What the hell happened?"

He was sporting a black eye, and a bruise was forming on his cheek, but perversely he was grinning like a kid at Christmas. Her fingers gently probed the abused skin, and he captured her wrist in his hand and pulled her close as he plastered her body to his own.

He kissed her fingertips, and she cocked her head to look at him, wondering how she was meant to stop herself falling in love with a man such as him.

He smiled. "Jack and I were sparring."

Lacey wasn't sure how to respond, but from the look on his face, she guessed this was a good thing. "This is good?"

Gunner lifted her up and twirled her around, making her throw her head back and laugh before he settled her on the counter and stepped between her legs. She was wearing a short green floaty skirt and a white vest top with flip flops which now hung from her feet.

"This is great. We sparred, and then the guys kicked my ass, and I kicked theirs a little bit, and it was like being home again. Do you know what I mean?"

Lacey felt her body soften as she leaned toward him so happy to see a genuine smile on his face and the weight of guilt lifting a little. "Yeah, Gunner, I understand."

She did, hadn't she been thinking the exact same thing earlier when he'd walked in?

"Do you know the crazy part?"

Lacey ran her hand over his cheek as he turned to kiss her palm. "No, I don't read minds."

"All I kept thinking about when I was there, and this weight was lifting, was that I couldn't wait to get back here and tell you about it."

"Gunner."

This man could break her so easily and not have a clue he'd done it. She had no doubt he would never knowingly harm a hair on her head, but it would be so easy to fall in love with him and then end up a shell when he walked away needing more fun in his life.

Gunner buried his head in her neck, his lips skimming the pulse in her neck.

"I mean it. As good as it feels to know I can maybe one day find my way back to them respecting me, the best feeling was coming home and seeing you."

Gunner was devastatingly handsome all the time, his ice-blue eyes, the blond hair and scruff and the wide shoulders but when he smiled like he was now, she had no defence against it.

"I'm so happy you had a good day, sweetheart."

"What about you? How was your day?"

His hands were on her waist his thumbs caressing the soft skin of her bare belly as he spoke, making it difficult to concentrate.

"Good."

"Just good?"

Lacey saw the sexy smirk as he drew back.

"Yeah. I talked with Skye, got some designs ironed out."

"Let's see if we can make it better than just good."

His lips came down on hers in a kiss that stole every thought from her head. The man could kiss like the very devil himself, and she wanted more. His teeth nipped at her lips, and she opened for him, letting his tongue caress her own as he made love to her with his mouth.

Lacey speared her fingers through his hair, gripping it hard as she clamped her legs around his back and held on. The next minute she was in his arms, her legs and arms around him as he held her by the curves of her ass and not breaking the kiss, he carried her upstairs and into the room they had shared last night.

All traces of the threat against her were gone, taken away by Eidolon, and now Gunner would erase any bad memories. He sat on the edge of the bed and kept her in place, the stony ridge of his cock pressing against her clit, making them both moan. The thin barrier of her knickers wet with the need for him.

Last night after the shock of finding the nightgown on her bed, he'd held her in his arms, but hadn't touched her as she wanted him too, like he was now. She felt a desperate edge to their lovemaking as he nipped at her neck, drawing her top over her head, and throwing it to the floor. Her nipples peaked in the lace bra, and she saw the look of carnal desire in his eyes that made her feel sensual and sexy in a way she never had before.

"So fucking beautiful."

Lacey grasped at his top, wanting to get her hands on all the warm muscular flesh beneath and he helped, lifting one bunched bicep behind his head, and pulling the shirt off in a fluid move she was sure boys learned in school to distract the opposite sex.

Gunner grasped her waist as he lay back and pulled her so that her sex was hovering over his mouth. Lacey suddenly felt shy, unsure, but his hands stroking the skin of her ass and his eyes never leaving her face gave her confidence as he silently asked for permission. Lacey moved the last bit and then she was in heaven, his mouth was on her, licking and kissing through the panties she wore.

Lacey threw her head back, letting him control the pace as she rode his face with abandon, not feeling embarrassed by how wet she was or how wanton but enjoying every sensation that flew through her body. The hands at her hips shifted, and in a strangely erotic move, he tore her panties from her, removing the scrap of lace so he could touch his tongue and lips to her clit. His beard rasped against the delicate skin of her thighs and pussy as her climax built until she couldn't hold it back and his name fell from her mouth as wave after wave of pleasure moved through her.

As her orgasm ended, he slowed his pace and he flipped her, so she was on her back still half-dressed with him poised above her, the evidence of her climax glistening on his face.

"You are the most stunning creature I have ever met."

He kissed her then, the taste of her desire between them adding to the eroticism of the moment. With a last kiss, he rose from the bed, his eyes not leaving her as she lay watching him undress.

"Lose the bra, Cosmo." Lacey unclipped her bra and went to remove the skirt too.

"No leave that, I like the idea of fucking you in that short flirty skirt. It's all I've been able to think about all day."

Lacey did as he asked, too distracted by the gorgeous man in front of her, who was so confident in his own skin. His cock was hard, the bead of pre-come on the tip as he took a condom from his pocket and covered himself.

She could watch him all day long and probably climax from just the sight of him touching his cock as he stroked it once and then moved to her. Nestling between her thighs, he braced his elbows on either side of her head and looked at her, and she wondered what he was thinking.

Then she was lost as he kissed her—slow, sensual, drugging her mind as he pushed into her slowly. The tempo of his lovemaking different now but no less devastating to her senses. The slight burn as he filled her adding to her pleasure as she wrapped her legs around his hips as he slid fully inside her.

Gunner stayed motionless for a second, just kissing her, seeming content to just be inside her. If it wasn't for the twitch in the muscles

65

at his shoulders as she held him, she would think he wasn't affected like she was.

"Gunner, I need you to move."

The sexy twitch of his lips was lethal to her equilibrium. If she could transfer that look to a model, she would be able to sell invisible suits. Her squirming encouraged him to move, and soon he was rocking into her slowly, his pelvis rubbing her clit every time until she was on the verge of another climax.

"Touch yourself, Lacey. Get there, I'm right behind you."

Lacey felt the blush heat her cheeks as she moved her hand between them, feeling the quiver of his abdominal muscles as she stroked her clit. The climax hit her hard and fast, dragging every sensation to that one spot, the feeling of him moving inside her making it so much more than ever before.

Gunner watched, his eyes on her the entire time, and then he buried his head in her neck as his own movements became jerky and he came. It was a strange feeling to have the barrier of latex between them after it not being there the first time. It didn't detract from the experience at all for her, but she wondered if it did for him.

Gunner collapsed onto the bed beside her and dragged her until she lay over his body, his arms around her. They remained silent for a few minutes then he lifted his head and looked down at her, his eyes warm and gentle.

"I need to get rid of this condom. Don't move." He kissed her nose and disappeared into the bathroom. Lacey watched the way his muscles bunched in his back and the sexy curve of his ass as he went.

"I feel you watching me, woman." His voice was teasing, and she liked it, but then she seemed to like everything about this man.

"I like watching you. It's not every day a woman gets a real live Viking in her bed."

Lacey turned on her side, the skirt still around her waist as he sauntered back from the bathroom, naked as the day he was born. It was hard not to admire that kind of beauty, not perfection—the scars on his body would never allow him to be traditionally perfect in the fake world of the media—but he was real perfection, each mark telling his story.

Gunner covered her body laughing. "Woman, stop objectifying my body. I'm not a piece of meat you know."

Lacey laughed as he hauled her into his arms and held her, so she was pressed against him and kissed her head.

"Oh, you're something all right."

Her hand on his chest was covered with his own, and he kissed her fingers as they lay quiet, just enjoying being together.

"I like this, just being here with you."

"I like you being here with me, too." Lacey could admit to herself that she was falling for him fast, but she didn't say it out loud not wanting to scare him off. Gunner had enough on his plate without the added pressure of her declaring her feelings for him. She wouldn't know for another ten days if their time together in Germany had created a child. Lacey wouldn't push him into a corner so that he had nowhere to go.

So many of Gunner's choices had been taken away from him and she wouldn't take any more from him. So, she'd enjoy what they had, and if they had made a child together, they would deal, and if not, it gave them different choices to make. She just hoped that whatever happened she didn't end up with a broken heart.

Chapter 11

Gunner trudged through the woods behind Lacey's house looking for more signs of the men who'd been watching and found nothing. True to their word, the men of Eidolon had come through and every night since the attack on Lacey's sanctuary there had been someone there at night.

He'd hardly left her side since that day, either. Choosing to do his work from there on a computer Will had set up for him in the spare room. Lacey had her home office, so it worked well. The two times he'd gone into Eidolon to make it seem to the two idiots watching him that he was indeed working his way back in, he'd left Lacey with either Evelyn or Roz and Kanan.

Roz might be heavily pregnant, but she was still the deadliest woman he knew, and he wouldn't cross her even now. Her husband Kanan was ex-MI5 and equally deadly. He now worked for Fortis Security, a friend of Eidolon's and their frequent ally.

Gunner looked up, trying to find Waggs, his former or maybe current teammate; he wasn't sure what the state of play was yet. They'd been treating him like they forgave him, but he could still sense the undercurrent of wariness in some, especially Blake. He understood it, probably more so now he had Lacey.

If anyone had watched her take the same beating that Pax had and not stopped it, he'd lose his damn mind. It was one of his biggest regrets, and he had a lot of them. He'd tried to apologise, but in truth Blake wasn't ready to hear it yet, and Gunner respected that.

Waggs stepped out in front of him, and he almost jumped out of his skin. The man was spooky the way he could just appear like that, and he was one hell of a medic. Each man on the Eidolon team owed him their life at least once.

"Fucking hell, Waggs, you scared the shit out of me."

Waggs had been the quickest to accept him back, and he would never betray that trust ever again, not any of them, he'd die first.

Waggs smirked and shrugged. "Losing your edge, Viking."

"Nah, just things on my mind."

"One of those wouldn't be a certain ex-model, would they?"

Gunner cocked his head. "That obvious?"

"Duh, you've hardly been discreet about it, but I wasn't sure if it was for the benefit of anyone watching from the Carmine camp or if it was real."

Waggs and Gunner continued walking through the woods toward the river, checking all the wires were in place and satisfied they were, began the walk back to the house.

"Oh, it's real, alright. I've never felt like this about a woman before."

Waggs angled to look at him. "I thought you two would get together at Skye and Nate's wedding, but then everything happened, and your life blew up."

"I think we might have, but I guess things happen for a reason."

"You believe that?"

Gunner shrugged. "I have to. Otherwise, all the shit that's happened is for nothing. If Lacey is my reward for surviving, then it's worth it. My penance is living with what I've done to those people I care about."

"You think that's enough? Just to live with what you've done and go on and have a perfect life with Lacey?"

Gunner stopped and focused on Waggs, seeing no condemnation or blame just a question in the other man's eyes.

"No, I don't and if there were a way to make what I did good then I would, but there isn't so I have to live my life as best I can. If I'm lucky enough to have a woman like Lacey care about me, don't I owe it to her to give the same back?"

"Yes of course and I'm not talking about you, I just mean in general. We all know you've punished yourself for what happened. Have you been to see Milla yet, since you got back?"

"No, I haven't had time."

Waggs just lifted his head but stayed silent. He knew the truth, so he didn't need Waggs to spell it out. He was ashamed to go and see her knowing that once again, her life had been affected by his actions.

"You should go."

"Yeah, I will when all this is sorted out."

They had reached the large back lawn now and were walking toward the house. Lacey waved at them through the office window, and he smiled, feeling his heart jump at the smile she gave him. He waved back and knew Waggs was watching him and didn't feel the slightest bit self-conscious.

He walked into the house and saw Waggs head around the side, blending back into the land surrounding the house and keeping watch. Taking the stairs two at a time, he headed to the office and grinned when he saw Lacey was on a video call with Skye. He tried to back out and give her privacy, but she turned.

"Gunner, Skye wants to know if we're free for dinner tomorrow night with her and Nate and Mitch and Autumn?"

"Come on, Gunner, say yes and let me interrogate you as a good friend should."

Lacey blushed and shot her friend a glare which he thought was adorable.

"If Lacey wants me there, then that's where I'll be."

Skye clapped her hands and smiled. "Yes. Lacey, I'll text you the details later. Now I have to go and scrub paint out of the fridge before Nate gets home and Nancy gives him those big eyes. I tell you, that child can literally wrap her daddy around her little finger."

"As it should be."

Skye got a dreamy, faraway look. "Yeah, you're right. Okay, catch you later."

Skye disappeared from the screen, and Lacey spun to look at him. "You sure you're okay with this? I don't want you doing something just to keep my friends happy."

"I'm sure, and she has an obligation as your friend make sure your man isn't a complete dickhead, at least to you."

Lacey stood and walked into his arms, resting her head on his shoulder. She looked tired which he knew in part was his fault from keeping her up at night making love, but the rest was stress and her working herself hard. He rubbed his hand over her back, before capturing her nape under the silky blonde hair she wore down today.

"You good, Cosmo?"

"Yeah, just feeling a little restless today."

"You want to go out? Maybe head into town for some lunch and walk around the shops?"

Lacey cocked her head. "You'd do that?"

"Cosmo, there's nothing I wouldn't do for you."

Her smile and the light in her eyes were worth any shopping trip. "Thank you."

She went up on tiptoes and kissed him, and he pulled her close, addicted to her taste before releasing her.

"Let's go before I change my mind."

Lacey giggled, and soon they were wandering around Hereford. He loved seeing his hometown through her eyes and the glee on her face when she saw the Cathedral in all its glory. He'd sold his house when everything had gone down with Osbourne, not feeling like he deserved a home here and believing he'd never be back. Being here with her was a minor miracle and one he was cherishing every second of.

Waggs was right; he didn't deserve to have this joy in his life, but he'd be a fool to turn his back on it. He'd do whatever he could to right his wrongs for his team, as he'd done with Milla and his grandmother. As selfish as it may be, walking away from Lacey wasn't something he could do.

They were in the Left Bank shop near the river paying for some artisan bread when he heard his name and froze.

"Gunner?"

He turned slowly and came face to face with Frederick Granger. His hand automatically tightened around Lacey's as he moved so she was slightly behind him. He had no idea what Granger's game was, but he didn't trust him in the slightest.

"Frederick."

"I hear you're working for my son again."

So that was his game, a fishing expedition to find out what was going on. Did that mean that the information he was passing to Bás wasn't getting through or that he was being kept out of the loop?

"Yes, it's early days but I think we're coming to an understanding."

Frederick was an elegant man, tall like his sons and fit from his army days with a formal, imposing bearing. Even now he wore a suit, no chance of him being caught in a pair of jeans. His hair had been dark like Jack's, and there was a definite resemblance, but his hair was now greying. Unlike Jack and Will, this man didn't have a shred of decency in him, and the concept of family meant nothing.

Gunner seethed to think what he'd put them all through. If he had his way, Frederick would be dead or locked up already, but he knew an operation like this needed careful handling and was happy to let Jack and Will take the lead seeing as this man had given them life.

"And who is this?" Frederick looked around Gunner at Lacey, and he tensed before relaxing, not wanting to give anything away.

Gunner turned slightly giving Frederick access to Lacey even though his instincts screamed for him not to do so. "This is a friend of mine, Lacey Cannon."

"Frederick Granger, Jack and William's dad. It's a pleasure to meet you, Lacey." He held out his hand and Gunner almost lost his mind when the man bent and kissed her hand as if it was a gallant gesture instead of the veiled threat it actually was. He pulled Lacey away and saw Frederick smirk knowingly.

"It's nice to meet you, Mr Granger."

"Please, call me Frederick."

Gunner wanted to puke as the smarmy bastard tried to charm Lacey. He just needed to get out of there and get her away from the man.

"We can't stop, we have a table booked."

"Well, I won't keep you. Stay safe and make sure you look after this young lady. The world is a dangerous place."

The threat was clear, and it made him want to turn around and throw Frederick Granger into the river below the bridge where they stood.

Gunner forced himself to walk slowly instead of running to the car and getting Lacey out of there.

"Was that really Jack and Will's father?"

"Yep."

"Hmm. I guess they get their charm from their mother then."

Gunner threw back his head and laughed as he ushered her into the car, cutting their trip short with no explanation and no consultation and she didn't bat an eyelid, seemingly understanding something wasn't right and not making a fuss.

"You're one quick cat."

Lacey smiled and buckled her seat belt. "At least we got the bread I've been fancying for dinner tonight. I thought we could have it with cheese and stuff in bed. Like a bednic instead of a picnic."

"Sounds perfect but I need to stop at Eidolon first. Are you happy to come with me or do you want me to drop you at home?"

"I'll come with you."

72

Gunner took her hand and kissed her palm before resting their hands on his thigh. "Good answer."

Chapter 12

Lacey had no clue what the undercurrent of hostility that had been radiating from Gunner had been about regarding Frederick Granger, but she trusted him and if he didn't trust him, then neither did she. Plus, she absolutely hated it when men thought they could kiss her without asking first. Although she had to concede that when Gunner did it, it was different.

Eidolon wasn't what she expected. It was so high tech it made her brain hurt. A guarded gate which meant someone had to buzz them in and cameras were watching their every move once they were inside.

"Eidolon does security for the Royals, right?"

Gunner drove around the back but glanced at her first. "Yes."

"This seems a little overkill for a security company." She waved her hand at the razor-wire fences and the cameras. "I mean the training course I get but the rest?"

Gunner parked next to a wicked-looking bike and a high-end Land Rover Discovery and then angled toward her. "I guess it is, but they do other stuff too."

"This other stuff. If you tell me will you have to kill me?" Lacey grinned as she tilted her head at him, teasing.

"Kind of, yes."

Lacey had her suspicions before, but now she knew that whatever they did was way more than just ensuring the safety of the Queen. Eidolon literally meant Ghost, and she realised they were a Ghost Ops team.

"Can I ask you one question?"

Gunner picked up her hand and rubbed his thumb over her knuckles. "You can ask me anything, Cosmo."

"Do you have multiple passports?"

Gunner looked surprised by her question, but then he chuckled. "Yes, Lacey, I have more than one passport."

"Okay. Enough said."

Her understanding now complete, it made her feel both better and worse. Better because she knew Carmine would never get past Gunner and worse because she realised that whatever had happened to put him in the middle of Eidolon, this mystery person was so much more deadly than she'd thought.

"We good?"

Lacey pursed her lips. "Yes, but promise me you'll be careful."

Gunner cupped the back of her head and brought her lips close to his, leaning his forehead against hers.

"You don't need to worry about me, Cosmo. I fucking love that you do. It makes me want to take you to bed and show you how much and in multiple ways, but you really don't need to worry."

"Okay, Gunner, I trust you to stay safe."

He took her lips in a soft kiss that stole her breath and left her wanting more when he pulled away.

"Camera's."

Lacey looked up and laughed. "Oops."

Gunner got out of the car and crossed to her side and grabbed her hand as they walked to the main doors where Liam was waiting with a smirk on his face.

"Caught you kids necking on the camera. Thought I was gonna have to rinse my eyes with bleach if Gunner got his todger out."

Gunner punched him in the shoulder as he passed, and Liam laughed harder.

"You're disgusting."

"So, Taamira tells me, but she loves me anyway."

Lacey caught the way Liam locked the door using his thumbprint and she followed Gunner and Liam through the hallway and past another door which had a retina scanner which Liam used to open the door. The protocols at this place were ridiculous, but after what she'd learned in the car, she now understood it a little better at least.

Once through the door, the place opened up into a series of offices, one of which Autumn was working in with baby Maggie on the floor at her feet. Lacey gave her a little wave, and Autumn waved back. Then she passed a gym with a full fitness suite including a treadmill, weights, benches, a climbing wall, and a massive boxing ring which was empty.

A smell of food hit her, and she remembered she hadn't eaten since last night. It was a regular occurrence for her to forget to eat, and then she would eat loads to catch up. It wasn't great, but she'd always been the same.

Still holding her hand Gunner walked her into a break room that was way more luxurious than any break room she'd been in. It had tables for eating, as well a couch, a television, and games station.

Lacey grinned when she saw Pax with Blake and Evelyn and Astrid sitting together.

"Hey, Lacey," Pax said, standing to greet her with a hug. Lacey hugged her back and let go of Gunner to sit.

"You okay to hang here while I talk to Jack a minute?"

"Yes, of course."

Blake stood suddenly making her jump. "What you want with Jack?"

"Blake!" Lacey caught the warning in Pax's voice as Blake moved in on Gunner.

Blake glanced back at Pax and then returned his glare to Gunner. The tension in the room had skyrocketed, and she didn't really understand why but suspected Blake had some sort of beef with Gunner still.

Blake looked at her, and she could see the anger burning him. "He tell you what he did?"

Pax stood, and the chair she was sitting on fell to the floor. "Blake! Enough."

Blake looked at the woman he clearly loved, and she could see he was torn.

"No, Pax it's not. It will never be enough. He watched while two men beat you and left you for dead and he did fuck all to stop it happening."

Lacey felt bile burn her throat at the words and her eyes shot to Gunner, wanting him to deny it, but she could see by the guilt in his eyes and the fact he made no move to defend himself that it was true.

"Is it true?" Lacey hated that her voice shook like it did and the quiver in her bottom lip as she barely held herself together. She could feel other people behind her and knew more had walked in the room and were watching her humiliation.

"Yes."

A sob burst from her, and she turned to Liam who was behind her. "Can you take me home, please?" She saw him look at Gunner, and then he nodded. "Sure, sugar, let's go."

Lacey kept her hand on her stomach to try and hold the sickness at bay until she could get some air. The room felt stifling and hot, and she knew it would only be minutes before she broke down.

Shouting from behind her made her turn to see Pax storm from the room with Blake following after her, but all she could see was the look of hurt on Gunner's face. It broke her heart that he was hurting, but she couldn't be with a man who could allow that to happen.

Liam guided her into his car, and she instantly missed the familiar scent of Gunner's ride.

Liam was silent until they got to her house. "Life is rarely as simple as black and white, Lacey. Blake was wrong to do what he just did."

"Was he lying?" Lacey desperately wanted Liam to say yes, but she already knew the answer because it was plastered on Gunner's face.

"No, but…"

Lacey shook her head. "No buts. I can't be with a man who would allow that. End of story."

Liam's jaw ticked, and she could see he wanted to say more, but he kept quiet. "Let's get you inside." Liam walked her in, and she turned at the door once he'd done a sweep of the house. "I'll be outside if you need me."

"Thank you, but I think I might try and get some sleep, it's been a busy week."

Liam shoved his hands in his pockets. "Okay, Lacey."

As soon as the door closed, she could feel the tears overwhelming her and barely made it upstairs to her bedroom that still smelled like Gunner before the tears came. She cried for what might have been, for Pax, for Milla, for herself and what she'd been building with Gunner that was now lost. Mostly she cried for him. He had so much good inside him, so much to give, but that was the one thing she couldn't forgive.

Her hand moved to her belly, and she wondered if a child grew inside her that would be dragged into this mess. She wished that she could say she didn't want that, but the truth was, no matter what Gunner had done she couldn't be with him. The stark truth was she loved him. Sometime in the last ten days, she'd fallen in love with a man she now realised she hardly knew. She'd thought he was a protector, but no protector would allow what he'd allowed to happen.

Lacey felt nausea bubble up again, and the pain in her head make her feel worse as she cried herself to sleep, allowing blessed exhaustion to render her unconscious from the pain and the grief.

Chapter 13

Gunner stood motionless watching the woman he at this moment realised he loved, walk away with Liam a look of betrayal and disappointment on her face.

"How could you, Blake?" Gunner turned to Pax who had grabbed hold of Blake's arm. "We both know he had no choice. If he'd intervened, they would have killed Milla, and she, unlike me, was completely helpless."

"He should have found a way." Blake looked less confident now, but Gunner didn't care. He closed down every emotion he had, allowing nothing to penetrate his now broken heart. He should go after her and try and explain, but Blake was right, he'd done those things. There was no defending himself. The best thing he could do for Lacey would be to stay away from her and let her live her life. If there was a child from their night in Germany, that would be different, but if not, he should walk away.

"Jack, I need to talk to you."

Jack was watching from the doorway, his arms crossed over his chest and a look of anger on his face. Gunner didn't know if it was directed at him or not, but right now, he didn't care. He just wanted to relay this information about his father and update him on the contact with Bás, and then he was going to find a bar and get blind drunk.

Lacey would be safe with Liam and Waggs. He trusted them to keep the woman he loved more than his own pathetic life safe from harm.

"Sure, follow me." Jack glanced at Alex. "Get everyone in the gym in twenty minutes, and I mean everyone except Liam and Waggs. Leave them on Lacey."

Alex dipped his head in agreement, and Gunner followed Jack back to his office.

"I'm sorry, Jack."

Jack leaned back on his desk, crossing his arms, and watched Gunner. "Why do you do that? Take the blame for everyone else when it isn't on you?"

"I don't."

"Yes, you do."

"Well, that was my fault."

"No, it wasn't. Blake has every right to be angry, but he doesn't have the right to do what he just did."

"He's hurting. I understand it, Jack. I would be the same if it was Lacey."

"Maybe but there are ways of doing something, and that fucking ambush wasn't it."

Gunner didn't know what to say to that, so he waited it out.

Jack sighed and uncrossed his arms. "What did you want to tell me?"

"I was in town with Lacey when your father approached us."

Jack's face turned to granite; the emotions impossible to read. Only the vibe of fury he was throwing off allowed any insight into how he was feeling.

"And what did dear old dad have to say?"

Gunner could hear the control and the strain in the simple, almost jovial sentence and braced. "Just that he was glad I was working for his sons again and that I should keep Lacey safe as the world was a dangerous place."

The air in the room suddenly seemed sucked of oxygen and then came the explosion.

"God damn motherfucker. I'm gonna kill him." Jack spun and swept everything off his desk in a rare show of temper. Gunner stepped back not sure what to do as Jack went on a rampage, throwing the chair across the room. The office door flew open, and Astrid stood in the doorway, looking shocked.

"What the fuck, Granger?"

"Get out, Astrid. I can't be doing with you right now."

"Tough shit, because I'm not leaving."

Gunner stepped up as Alex came running.

"What the hell happened?" Alex glanced at Gunner with a frown, seeking answers to why their boss looked ready to commit murder.

"Everybody, get the fuck out of my office. Now."

Alex and Gunner paused, then backed away, but Astrid didn't move.

"You should leave." Alex touched Astrid on the arm, and she pulled away.

"You go. I'll be there in a second."

Jack was silent, leaning on the table with his back to them, breathing hard and Gunner could see he was struggling. He would be too. To know that your own parent hated you enough to try and take everything from you must be difficult at best.

Alex shrugged, and Gunner followed him out as he closed the door. They both knew Jack would never lay a finger on Astrid or any other woman for that matter, and maybe having someone who wasn't Eidolon or family to stand with him was what he needed.

"What happened?" Gunner had his hands in his pockets as they moved down the hallway. They stopped at the door of the gym where everyone was waiting for Jack to come out and ream them a new asshole. To say he was angry was an understatement. Gunner avoided everyone's eyes, not wanting to get into a conversation about what happened with Lacey or Jack. He had no idea if Jack had told the team about his father, but that wasn't his news to tell.

"Listen, Alex, not to be a dick, but you need to ask Jack that. Whatever I told him is his to share or not. I just want to get the hell out of here."

Gunner could feel the eyes of the others on him, and it made his skin itch. He wanted out of there before he did or said something he'd regret.

"Blake was out of line, but he's sore over it."

Gunner looked up at his old teammate. It was becoming ever more apparent that he wouldn't be able to slip back into the team he'd once loved and betrayed. "I get it, Alex, I do. I did some bad shit to you guys, and I can't take it back. I don't expect forgiveness or redemption. I just want to get this shit done so I can move on."

Alex raised his eyebrows. "You won't be coming back?"

Gunner gave a humourless laugh. "How can I, man?"

Alex stayed quiet, having no more answers than he did.

"Look, tell Jack he knows how to reach me, and I'll be in touch."

Gunner went to walk away, and Alex grabbed his arm. "You got someplace to stay?"

He didn't. He hadn't bothered to sort somewhere, and then he'd been with Lacey. Just the thought of her made his chest ache. He wouldn't admit that to Alex, though. It was about time he remembered that the only person he should rely on was himself. His team were gone, at least for him they were.

"Yeah, I'm good."

Gunner shook off the arm and walked out of the building to his car. He got in and gripped the steering wheel hard. The car smelled like her, the soft scent swirling around him in the warm heat of the August afternoon. Just an hour ago, he'd been happier than he could ever remember being, and now it was all gone. Swept away like dust on the wind and he could blame nobody but himself.

He wondered if his choices would always be in the way of his future and knew they would. Some things you could not walk away from, and his decisions to let Pax be beaten and help Callie be kidnapped were some of them. It didn't matter that he didn't have a choice, Blake was right. He should have found a way.

Starting the car, he headed into town to find a bar and get so drunk it didn't matter where he slept. He just needed to forget the shit show his life had become. He was tired, so very tired of fighting all the time.

He left his car, a loaner from Eidolon, in the carpark near the football ground and headed into the old part of the town. The newly developed Old Market was full of shops and eateries, but he just needed a good old-fashioned pub where he could sit at the bar and get drunk without anyone bothering him.

Walking into the Litchfield Vaults, he breathed in the smell of beer and welcomed the darkness of the bar. Sitting on a stool, he ordered a double Vodka straight. When the barmaid brought it over, she gave him a flirty smile which he returned for just a fraction of a second before a sense that he was betraying Lacey by even smiling at the other women overcame him and he shut it down.

Knocking back the drink, he lifted his finger for another. "Keep them coming."

"No problem, handsome."

Swirling the clear liquid, he wondered if Lacey was okay. Was she upset or did she consider she'd had a lucky escape? He almost wished for the second because the thought of her in pain made his heart ache. He would do anything not to have hurt her. He'd known the full truth about some of what he'd done, or not done in some cases, would hurt her and he wondered now if it was why he'd avoided the details.

Was he so desperate that he had to hide his true self to get the woman he wanted? Probably, but it had worked for a short time, and he couldn't regret it. His time with Lacey had shown him how life could have been. Given him a glimpse into what he might have had, and he would treasure it. But the pain of losing her was almost too much to bear, and he had no clue how Alex had done it, mourning Evelyn for so long.

He could feel his thoughts becoming jumbled as he knocked back glass number four or was it five? He didn't remember, but the pain was easing, which was good. He'd never been a big drinker, but he could see the appeal as things became numb.

Chapter 14

Jack knew the second the door closed on Gunner and Alex that Astrid had completely ignored him. The stubborn woman had no sense of self-preservation and getting under his skin and winding him up seemed to be her sole mission in life. But right now, he wasn't sure he could hold himself in check as he should.

The anger burning inside him was consuming him to the point he couldn't sleep, couldn't think straight. His control on everything was slipping, his team were fighting amongst themselves, his father wasn't even hiding his misdeeds any longer, and the threat to the Palace became more viable every day.

"Go, Astrid."

She was the one person he couldn't be around. His attraction for the irritating woman was at odds with how annoying he found her. She was beautiful, no doubt about that, smart, sexy, funny, but she was also reckless and wild, and he had no place in his life for that.

"No."

Jack spun around so fast, pinning her to the door with his body, his breath coming fast as he looked down into the stunning unique eyes of the woman who made his blood boil. A ring of aqua green blending into almost amber in the middle, they had captivated him from the beginning.

Jack grasped her wrists in his hands, holding them against the door, the feel of her soft body against his hard one a torturous pleasure.

"Get the fuck out before I do something we'll both regret."

The little minx licked her bottom lip and pushed against him, making him fight to hold back the moan.

"How do you know what I'll regret? You don't know the first thing about me."

"I know you like to live dangerously, that you love the thrill of danger, that one day you're going to wind up dead because you don't know when to back down."

Astrid smiled, and it made his cock ache to push inside her and ride all that wild sexiness until she was a pile of satisfied woman lying over him. Then maybe she would be too exhausted to go out looking for danger.

"I see you listed all my best qualities."

Jack shook his head and stroked his finger down her cheek, relishing the satin feel of her peaches and cream skin so at odds with her ballsy attitude. She looked like an English rose with her blonde hair, willowy figure, and blush pink lips, but she had the mouth of a sailor and the grit of an army commander.

"You're a mystery in some ways, but I see the death wish, Astrid. The way you flirt with danger."

He sucked in a breath when she bit down on the finger he was using to stroke her face. Sucking the digit into her mouth like she was starving, laving it with her tongue to soothe the pain. His dick was now screaming for the release he knew he could find with her. Astrid wanted him, she'd made no secret of it, and against his better judgement, he wanted her too. He'd stayed away, wanting nothing to do with the hate fuck she wanted.

He and Astrid were like oil and water; they didn't mix well at all. Except between the sheets, he knew there they'd be spectacular.

He was two seconds from making a huge mistake when a bang on the door behind him brought him back from his insanity.

"Jack, everyone is in the gym waiting for you."

He pulled back, turning away as if he'd been burned and glared at the woman who'd woven her witchcraft on him.

"I'll be out now." His voice at least sounded normal even if his body and emotions felt anything but.

"You know, Jack, you should lighten up, have some fun, it might be good for you."

The words he'd heard all his life, about lightening up made him react. He turned to her with a sneer. "What? With you? No thanks." He knew the second the words left his mouth they'd been the wrong thing to say and expecting her anger, he was gutted when he saw the pain he'd caused flash across her features before she buried it deep and gave him a one-shouldered shrug.

"Nah, not me. I'll never let you touch me, Jack."

He stayed rooted to the spot as she put her hands in her jacket pockets and spun, leaving him standing there feeling like he'd just made a colossal mistake and having no idea how to fix it or even if he wanted too.

Rubbing his eyes, he realised he felt calmer than he had before his altercation with Astrid. Less like he was out of options with no way to stop the free fall. Managing to gather the threads of his control, he looked around at his trashed office ashamed that he'd done such damage in a fit of rage at the man who was meant to be his protector but was, in fact, his enemy.

It was a bitter pill to swallow but one he had to take, nevertheless. Righting his chair, he knew it was time to go out and fix the mess his team was becoming, and that started with him being honest.

He walked into the gym and looked around as the six men talking in hushed tones as they waited for him, went silent. Blake, Reid, Lopez, Decker, Alex, and Mitch. The others were on duty with Lacey, but he didn't see Gunner.

He folded his arms to keep his anger at bay. "Where's Gunner?"

"He left."

He looked at Alex in question. "I thought I made it clear I wanted every member of this team here."

Alex looked at Mitch and back to Jack. "We didn't realise Gunner was back on the team and neither, it seems, did he."

Jack rubbed his brow where a headache was forming.

"Then let me make it clear for you now. Gunner is a member of this team, and if anyone doesn't like it," he pointed behind him at the exit, "then the door is that way. This is my team, and I say who is on it and who is not. I understand the bad blood won't dissolve overnight and wrongs will need to be worked through but what happened today is not how we do things." He was looking directly at Blake as he spoke.

"Gunner did some awful things that resulted in people we care about getting hurt, but I need you all to take a deep hard look at yourselves. Would you have done anything differently, having met his sister and seeing how vulnerable she is? I know I wouldn't have. It's easy to judge and hold on to anger and rage but be honest with yourselves. If he'd really felt like we had his back, he would've found a way to tell us. Fuck, he would have told us about Milla."

Jack moved to the boxing ring and climbed up under the ropes into the middle.

"Gunner let us down, but we fucking let him down too. Not one of us is innocent, and we need to stop acting like hurt little bitches

86

and accept that. Now, does anyone have anything they want to say on this matter? Because for the love of God, if I have to discuss it again like we're a fucking sewing circle, then heads will roll."

The room was silent, and he could see that he was getting through to them when Mitch chuckled. He'd always been the calmest member of the team. Blake could be a hot head sometimes, and he'd seen the state Pax had been in after her attack, so he got it, but so did Gunner. What Blake had done was cruel and unfair.

"I'm all good, boss man."

"Lopez?"

"Sure, you're right. I would've done the same in his boat."

"Decker?"

"You know my feelings already." Jack did know how Decker felt. The profiler had been the one to point it out to him and hold a mirror up to the failings of the team allowing this to happen.

"Alex?"

"If I can work with Bás, I can work with Gunner." Bás was an altogether different kettle of fish; he'd been the one to beat Evelyn, albeit holding back, while undercover.

"Reid?"

Reid was quiet, but he adored Callie his girlfriend, and had been furious at Gunner for his involvement.

"Honestly, Callie and I were talking about this, and the fact is, she would've been in much more danger if he hadn't been involved. I don't like it, but it won't change how I work. Will it take me a little while trust him again?" He shrugged. "Probably, but I expect that goes both ways."

"Blake?"

Blake had his arms crossed over his chest, looking mutinous. "She needed to know the truth."

"Don't try and defend it, Blake. It was a dick move, and you know it. It was his to tell, not yours, and you went in with the sole purpose of hurting him and in the process hurt Lacey too."

"That wasn't my intention."

"Maybe not, but it was the outcome. Gunner knows he made mistakes, and God knows he's been busting his ass to fix them, but you're not innocent either, Blake, none of us are. So quit acting like a victim. We have an enormous mountain to climb with this threat, and we can't afford for us to be fighting. Can you work with Gunner or not?"

"I can try, for Pax and the team, I'll try."

Reid chuckled. "If the way Pax walked out of here is any indication then you have at least a week on the sofa." Blake rolled his eyes but didn't disagree.

"Good. Now I'm sure you're all wondering why I trashed my office. Well, Gunner found out who the third man working with Osbourne is, and it's Frederick Granger." He held up his hands to stop the talking that began.

"I can assure you, neither Will nor I knew about it. But we did have an issue before. The first Op we did taking out Miqdaad al-Sadir was because I had intel that my father was working with him and we wanted to put a stop to that. We thought it was over, but unfortunately, it's not. He's now working with both Osbourne and Samir al-Sadir. In exactly what capacity and how deep, we don't know. But my father was the one behind Milla's kidnapping. He's the man who targeted Gunner and therefore us."

"Gunner told you this?" Mitch asked.

"Yes, he was the one who brought me the information, but he sat on it until he was absolutely sure because he didn't want to blow my world to smithereens. My father is the enemy here, not Gunner. He was a pawn they selfishly used to weaken us, and they've succeeded as proved today. I understand if you have questions and I'll answer them as best I can."

"What's the plan, boss?" Blake asked, and he could tell he was getting through to them.

"I have a meeting with James Fitzgerald next week, and I think we need to bring the Queen in on this herself. We have no clue who we can trust on this except those two, and then we form a plan from there. But be aware my father has threatened Lacey if Gunner doesn't follow through on what they want. Let's make sure we have his back this time, even though he probably won't want it."

"Is Carmine still a problem for her?" Alex had caught Lacey when she'd collapsed after the kidnapping and attack, and they all liked the woman a lot. Plus, she was Skye's best friend, and Nate and Skye were Fortis and therefore friends.

"Carmine is still in jail, but he's had a few visitors of late including his brother and his legal counsel." Lopez had been monitoring Carmine Russo since they had found nightwear on Lacey's bed. It could well be the Russo family, but he also wouldn't put it past his father to use that to scare the woman.

"Check if there are any connections between Frederick and the Russo family. There isn't one I know of, but it's becoming clear that I don't know the man who fathered me at all."

"Is your mom safe with him?"

Jack could tell Reid hadn't wanted to ask, but it was a good question. "Yes, the one thing my father would never do is lift a finger to our mother. But I'll go around there later and make sure she's safe. Unfortunately, we can't move on him because if we do, the whole thing becomes too precarious. We need intel and a plan first, so I can't warn my mother, but she's out a lot with her friends. While we're here, I want to do some drills ending with randori in the ring."

He heard the groans. Drills were a killer, and randori was where you were attacked on all sides from all angles in quick succession and had to fight your way out of it. It was good exercise and why his men could hold their own in any situation.

"Quit whining and get changed."

"Someone should check on Gunner. He was pretty upset." Mitch was already in sparring gear.

"Good idea. Blake, you go. You fucked it, you fix it."

Blake didn't argue, just turned and left. As he did, Mitch moved up to Jack. "That wise?"

"Yep, they need to iron this out between them and forcing it is the best way to clear the air."

"Hope you're right, boss."

Jack didn't say it, but he did too, or they were all dead.

Chapter 15

Lacey applied the last swipe of mascara to her eyelashes and sat back from the mirror at her vanity to check the overall appearance. Clever make-up tricks she'd learned from the experts now hid the smudges under her eyes, the evidence of her heartbreak. She'd spent the first day after her break up with Gunner in bed crying and then she'd dragged her ass out of bed. Wallowing in self-pity would get her nowhere.

Now a week later, she was feeling a little more human at least. Her grief at his loss turning to mild depression. Her heart still ached when she thought about Gunner, which was why she'd tried to stay busy working and had even travelled to London to oversee the photo shoot for next spring's children's range. Waggs had been a good sport about it, and she found him good company, but his mannerisms were so like the man she'd fallen for, it made her miss Gunner more.

Her plan for today was to work from home, but she'd always taken care of herself and saw no reason to stop now just because she worked from home and was nursing a broken heart, so she'd made an effort to put on her face and dress in something fun. A yellow-spotted tie sleeve dress with a vee neck and buttons down the front that fell to her knees made her feel happier. Clothes had always been her way of making herself feel better. Certainly when she was with Carmine it had been the only thing she could control and, in the end, he'd taken that too.

Not like Gunner, he'd looked at her with desire and more no matter what she wore or didn't wear. He'd never put a single second of pressure on her or told her she was lacking. All he'd done was make her feel like she was the most beautiful woman in the world. That in itself didn't mean a lot to her, beauty was a perceived subject in her book. It was the way he made her feel strong, like they were partners, that had made her fall for him. Even in moments when she was weak, he never made her feel that way.

Lacey jumped when her phone that was sitting by the bed rang, and she moved to answer it, quickly, smiling when she saw Skye's name. Her friend had shown up the second night after the-break-up-that-wasn't-really-a-break-up because they hadn't actually been together. A tub of ice-cream later the entire sorry story lay bare between them and a carton of chocolate chunk had been decimated.

"Hey, hun."

"Hi. Guess who gave birth to a bouncing baby boy this morning?" Lacey could hear the excitement in her friend's voice, and it was infectious as she felt the grin pull at her cheeks in happiness.

"Oh my God, did Roz have her baby?"

"Yep, early hours of this morning, two weeks late and he's a bruiser, nine pounds three ounces."

"Ouch, that makes me want to cross my legs. What did they call him?" Lacey relaxed back against the headboard and crossed her ankles.

"I know. I thought Noah was bad at seven-pound five. They decided on Deacon for a name."

"Awe that's so sweet, and they're both okay?"

"Yeah, mum and baby are doing fine. Not sure about Kanan though. He turned up here afterwards and had that traumatised look on his face like he'd come from a war zone."

"Yeah, it must be hard for the men too, seeing the women they love in pain."

"I know Nate struggled with it. Anyway, I wondered if you wanted to go see them later? Apparently Roz needed a few stitches and had some bleeding, so they're keeping her in a for a few days until her iron levels are up nearer normal."

"Yes, I'd love that. I need to pick up a gift for her and the baby though. What time is visiting?"

"Two until four. I can pick you up around one-thirty?"

"Sounds good, see you then."

Lacey hung up with a smile on her face. Roz had turned out to be an unsuspected friend, and despite her fearsome reputation as an assassin, Lacey saw through that to the woman who loved her family. She was so happy she now had that family, complete with the son she'd admitted she wanted.

Lacey walked to the back door and looked out to see if she could find out who was on duty today. Personally, she thought it was overkill having such highly trained men watching over her when she was sure they had better things to do.

She was surprised to see Jack walking toward her with a grin on his face. He was disgustingly handsome, and what made it worse was he had no idea and probably didn't care. That was like catnip to most women except her, her heart and attraction was firmly in camp Viking.

"Morning, Lacey."

Lacey crossed her arms as she stepped back from the door to let him inside.

"Morning, Jack. I see I warranted the big guns today."

Jack chuckled. "No, I just had something else I needed Waggs to do, and the others are busy."

"I'm sorry if I'm causing problems. I can hire private security if you think I still need it."

They were standing by the back door, and she saw Jack clench his jaw, but when he looked up at her any sign of anxiety or stress was gone.

"No need and you're not causing any problems at all."

Lacey felt sure he was lying, after all Eidolon weren't a security company like most were, but she let it go. Jack didn't seem like the sharing type, and honestly, she had enough on her plate without looking for trouble.

"I have to pop into town and get a gift for Roz and Kanan."

Jack grinned and turned. "Baby shopping it is. I heard she had a little boy?"

Lacey was surprised as they chatted on the way to town how open Jack was. He'd admitted he and Roz had a somewhat complicated relationship because they both felt their operatives were the best. Still, with more than one of their team members being in relationships with each other, they had mostly buried the hatchet.

Lacey picked out the cutest onesie for the baby and some gorgeous pamper kits for the new mum. She'd think of something for Kanan, but she wanted the girls to have something too and bought them both a small gift.

Once back home, Jack went back to his post, blending into the tree line of her property like a phantom and Lacey wrapped the gifts with pretty paper and ribbons. She always liked wrapping presents and was sure she'd love doing it for her own family one day. Whether that would ever happen for her, she had no clue.

It had taken everything she had not to do an early pregnancy test. She just had to wait and see what happened. That didn't stop the dread every time she went to the bathroom though which was crazy. A baby was the last she needed right now and especially given the circumstances she found herself in. Yet, she'd be lying if she didn't admit that at this point she dreaded her period more than a positive test.

At one-twenty, Nate and Skye arrived to pick her up and Jack came over and had a hushed conversation with the man. Lacey tried to ignore it, but she was curious and wanted to know why Eidolon was so involved in her safety. She was soon distracted as they got to the hospital.

"I'll stay out here and grab a coffee, let you girls have some time with Roz." Nate leaned in and kissed Skye, and while it wasn't pornographic, it was certainly not a tame kiss. Lacey felt a pang of envy steal into her heart and hated herself for it.

"Ready?"

Skye hooked her arm through Lacey's, and she forced a smile onto her face that became genuine the second she saw Roz. She was lying in the bed, looking almost as white as a sheet, and had the most beatific smile on her face as she held her son in her arms.

Lacey knew Roz wasn't a hugger, but she didn't care and leaned in for a one-armed hug. "Congratulations."

Skye did the same, and then they both peered down at the perfect little angel in Roz's arms. He was the image of his father in every way except for his mouth, which was the same cupids bow as Roz.

"Oh, Roz, he's precious."

Roz looked down at her sleeping son, and the love was evident to see. "Little shit left my vagina looking like a meat grinder got hold of it, my belly is like a bowl of jelly, my boobs are like rock hard balloons sitting on my chest that leak every time I move, and I've never been happier."

Lacey laughed at her words remembering Skye saying similar things if not quite so colourful about the aftereffects of birth.

"I was going to ask how you are feeling, but I guess that sums it up nicely."

"Would you like to hold him?"

She raised a brow at the offer but immediately nodded. Roz turned and handed Deacon to her as Skye smiled and handed Roz the gifts they'd brought. Lacey was overwhelmed as the tiny bundle settled in her arms as his fingers stretched and grabbed her pinkie.

At that moment she realised how much she wanted this for herself, whether it was now or later on she wanted to be a mother. Deep down, she wanted that to be with Gunner, but she couldn't see a way forward after what had transpired between them. Perhaps mother nature had already chosen, and a deeply hidden part of her wanted that to be the case.

She had the strangest feeling of being watched, and as she lifted her head, her eyes locked on the handsome face of the man she loved. It was the look on his face that ruined her though, tearing a hole on the seams where she'd patched her broken heart. His eyes were soft as they rested on her and Deacon and so full of grief almost but also something else she couldn't quite contain.

Chapter 16

Gunner had no clue why Roz had sent him a text to ask him to come to the hospital and see her after she'd just given birth to her son, but he predicted it had something to do with Pax. Roz was ridiculously protective of her girls, considered them family, with her acting as the terrifying patriarch.

Walking around the corner and seeing Lacey holding a newborn had been like a punch to the gut. The look of wonder on her face as she cradled the infant in her arms made him want things he knew were lost to him. He'd do anything to go back and make things right with her. He knew in his heart that she was his one chance at something special, something that only came once in a lifetime if you were lucky.

She was it for him, the love of his life and he'd screwed that up too. Looking for the answers in the bottom of a bottle for three days hadn't helped either, so he'd gone hunting. Looking for Carmine Russo who he'd just learned had been given bail, a power-play by Osbourne no doubt to control him. A reminder of who was in charge, but Gunner was done being a puppet he was going on the offensive. If he found Carmine first, there'd be no question of him walking away and having a second chance at hurting Lacey, not while he still breathed.

Lacey looked up, and he saw the joy on her face at seeing him and then it was quickly doused with confusion.

Roz followed Lacey's gaze. "Ah, Gunner, thanks for coming."

Gunner pulled his eyes away from the woman who held his heart and looked at Roz, the leader of the Zenobi group. "Why am I here, Roz?"

Roz crossed her arms and glared at him, no less deadly after giving birth hours earlier than she was before her pregnancy.

"Tell her."

Gunner shook his head, confused. "What?"

"Tell Lacey why you let those men hurt Pax."

Gunner could feel the anger surging through him to have been put on the spot once again.

Lacey sat up and moved to hand the baby back to his mother. "Roz, I don't think this is a good idea."

"It's a perfect idea. Gunner seems hell-bent on sabotaging whatever you two have."

Gunner crossed his arms to keep from reaching for Lacey. "I think you'll find Blake did that."

"Blake was a dick, and he knows it, but you're no better. Not fighting for Lacey when you appear to care about her."

"I do care." He could feel his jaw flex so hard he thought it might crack.

"Prove it, tell her."

Gunner saw Lacey fighting to hold on to her emotions and cursed Roz for interfering.

"Excuse me. I need to use the ladies room." Lacey rushed past him, her scent leaving a hole in his heart as she swept past without even looking at him, Skye rushing after her. He itched to go after her, to hold her and tell her it would be okay, that he would fight her demons, but he was her demon in that minute, and that was like a stake through his chest.

"That was out of line, Roz."

"Was it? Because to me, it seemed like the perfect time for you to tell her that the only reason you let those men hurt Pax was because they had a gun to your sisters head."

He'd no intention of reliving those brutal minutes watching Pax get hurt knowing physically he could stop it, but it would end up with Milla getting hurt in ways he couldn't allow.

"It still happened, Roz, and I can't expect Lacey to accept that."

Roz softened her face as much as she could, and for a second, he could see what Kanan saw in the force of nature that was Roz.

"Lacey needs to realise that life isn't black and white, it has shades of grey with shadows, and that's where men like you live. Pax doesn't blame you now she knows the truth, and Lacey needs to understand that."

"Lacey needs to get on with her life and forget me."

Roz threw up her hand in frustration. "Honestly, you can't educate stupid. Fine, go. Leave and let the best thing that ever happened to you walk away without a fight. Show her that she isn't even worth that."

Roz turned from him, dismissing him as her son began to fuss. Gunner didn't hang around, instead of heading out into the hallway and looking for where Lacey might have gone. Seeing the ladies room door, he headed that way and without thinking walked inside, glad it was empty except for Lacey and Skye.

Lacey's tear-filled eyes met his in the mirror, and he saw her lip wobble and could no more hold back from taking her in his arms than he could stop breathing. Striding forward he pulled Lacey from Skye and wrapped his arms around her. Her body moulded to his, the soft curves made to fit him as she grasped his shirt at the chest and buried her head in his neck just under his chin.

In that time and place, it was as if everything that was wrong became right with the world. He held her while she cried and saw Skye slip from the room leaving the two of them alone. His guilt at bringing her to this place wrecked him, and he'd do anything to stop her tears.

"Please don't cry, Cosmo. You're killing me here."

His words seemed to have the opposite effect, and she cried harder.

"Do you want me to go?" It would kill him, but if it were what she wanted, he'd leave and hand her over into the arms of her best friend and her husband.

Relief flooded him when she shook her head and sobbed. "No."

"Tell me what's wrong and I'll fix it." Gunner knew he was making promises he may not be able to keep, but right now, he'd make a bargain with the devil to keep her tears at bay. She mumbled something against his chest, the vibrations making his dick harden and then he felt like an asshole for thinking about sex when she was so upset.

Gunner pulled back, wrapping his hand around her ponytail, and tugging her head back so he could hear her properly and caught sight of the tear stains on her cheeks. "I didn't hear that, Cosmo. What did you say?"

Her cheeks went pretty pink. "I got my period."

It took him a second to realise what her words meant, and when they registered, he had the biggest feeling of grief swamp him for what might have been.

Her tears gave him hope. "And this made you cry?"

Lacey swiped at her face, and he gently pushed her fingers aside so he could soak up her tears with his lips. He'd kiss away her tears for a lifetime if things had been different.

"I guess this was my last chance and I know I shouldn't admit this, especially to you, but I wanted us to have made a baby. That is so fucked up, isn't it?"

Gunner lifted his head from her cheeks. "No, not at all. I feel sad, too. A child with you would've been the best thing to ever happen to me. My son or daughter would've been blessed to have you as a mother."

"I thought you'd be relieved."

"No, not relieved, Cosmo, but for you, this may be for the best. Now you have a clean slate and can do anything you want to do without me like a noose around your neck."

"Don't say that." She gripped his biceps as her sadness receded, and he saw her fight return.

He loved Lacey in all her different moods but when she got that look in her eye it took everything in him not to lay her on the floor of this public ladies' room and fuck her silly.

Gunner released her from his hold and stepped back to grab her some tissues, not trusting himself to hold her a second longer without falling to his knees and begging her to forgive him.

"Here." He handed her the tissues, and she turned to the mirror and gasped at the black smudges of mascara under her eyes.

"Argh, I look like a racoon."

Gunner's lips tipped up at the corner. "A beautiful racoon."

Lacey caught his eyes in the glass. "Is that even a thing?"

Gunner shrugged as he shoved his hands in his pockets. "If it is you got it down."

He looked at his feet not wanting to leave but not having a reason to stay now she'd got herself under control.

"Gunner?"

His eyes met hers as she turned toward him. "Yes?"

"What did Roz mean about telling me?"

Gunner shook his head. "It doesn't matter. It won't change anything." He couldn't allow himself to get his hopes up that she might find a way to forgive him.

Lacey stepped forward and brushed his forearm with her fingers, and it sent blood straight to his cock. "Will you tell me anyway? Please?"

He could no more deny her than walk on the moon.

Gunner took her hand and kissed the tips of her fingers. "I'll tell you but not here. How about I come around later, and we can talk?"

"I'd like that."

His phone ringing broke the spell he found himself under, and he took it from his pocket seeing Bás's name. "I have to take this, but shall I come over around seven and bring takeout?"

Lacey nodded. "Sounds good."

Gunner wanted to kiss her, but he didn't have the right anymore, so he dipped his head, squeezed her hand to let her know how much her wanting to know meant to him and left. He passed Skye on the way out and stopped beside her and Nate.

Skye was watching him warily, and he didn't blame her. She'd had Lacey's back more than anyone else, and he was so glad for it.

"Jack tell you about Carmine?"

Nate looked at Skye who paled. "Yeah, he told me."

"I'm coming over to see Lacey tonight. We need to talk, and I have some explaining to do. Let me tell her?"

Nate cocked his head as if assessing him and then nodded. "Fine."

"You'll stay with her until she's covered?"

"Of course. Lacey is family to me."

The warning was clear. Nate was his friend, but Lacey was more than that, and he'd kick Gunner's ass if he hurt her again. Gunner lifted his chin to acknowledge the silent unsaid threat, even respecting   it   and   left.

99

Chapter 17

Lacey closed the door and slid the lock into place. Today had been an emotional rollercoaster, and she needed a couple of hours to get herself together before Gunner came over. She hadn't planned for this. Holding Deacon and then Gunner arriving had been a lot but then going to the bathroom and finding out her period had arrived had felt like a blow.

Turning to Gunner had been the most natural thing in the world, the feel of his arms instantly making her feel stronger and more able to cope but it also made her miss him more and question her decision to turn her back on him so quickly.

Like the true gentleman he was, he hadn't made her work for it when she'd asked if they could talk, he'd simply accepted it. Lacey shivered a little as the cooler air that had blown through earlier this week tickled her neck.

She loved this house but the feeling of safety that she'd had when she'd bought it wasn't the same now that someone had been inside it. Everything felt tainted even though she knew there was no way it could be Carmine.

Deciding to take a bath to try and relax, Lacey turned on the tap in her master bath and poured some of the honey milk bubbles under it, watching as the steam rose fragrant with the scent. Undressing, she pulled her hair back into a bun on her head and pulled up a relaxing playlist on her phone.

The jitters in her belly were from too much stress, and it dawned on her she could finally have a glass of wine which was precisely what the doctor ordered. She didn't need to get completely pissed, but a nice buzz might take the edge off. Turning off the water, she ran downstairs and grabbed a glass and bottle of Riesling from the fridge before taking it back upstairs.

Pouring a decent sized glass, she shed her robe and sunk down into the water, hitting play on her iPhone, and letting the sounds of Lewis Capaldi and the fruity German wine relax her tight muscles.

The light from outside was still bright as the last day of August drifted away, and she knew it would be thoughts of summer which consumed her now. Her brain was always out of sync with the seasons, looking forward to whatever line she would create next.

Cocking her head, she froze as she heard a sound in the bedroom. Her heart began to hammer in her chest as her belly clenched and she froze, unable to move. Listening intently for the sound to come again, she let out a loud breath and laughed when she heard the sounds of the immersion heater clicking on.

This was her first bath in the house since she'd bought it, preferring showers until now and she must have emptied the tank, meaning the heater kicked in. She heard danger where there was none. Her relaxing bath now ruined, she got out and wrapped a towel around her body before entering the bedroom.

Drying off quickly she put on some yoga pants, and a vest top and went downstairs, her glass still in her hand. Placing it on the kitchen island, she got out her sketch pad and went back into the living room and curled up on the couch to sketch out some ideas for a boy's summer range.

It was hard not to picture Deacon when she did it, the cute bundle enough to inspire anyone. Her phone rang, and she smiled to see Taamira's name. The princess had become a good friend in the last few weeks, often showing up when Liam was on duty to work on designs with her.

"Hey, Taamira."

"Hello, Lacey, I hope I am not disturbing you?"

Lacey placed the pad on the sofa by her feet and took a sip of wine. "Of course not. What can I do for you?" Lacey had learned that Taamira never called unless there was a reason.

"Well, I was wondering if you would be interested in a girl's night next week with Evelyn, Callie, Pax, Autumn, and me? Nothing fancy. It will be at my place and each of us brings a dish we made."

"I don't know. This sounds very much like a wives or girlfriend's thing."

"Oh, please say you'll come."

"Did Pax put you up to this?"

Silence met her and Lacey had her answer.

"Yes, but I was going to ask anyway. We would really love you to come. Please say yes?"

Lacey considered it. She had no idea what would come of this conversation with Gunner, but she owed it to herself to make this new life work and that involved embracing every opportunity that came her way, especially when it was the hand of friendship.

"Fine, are we going healthy or full-on food porn?"

Taamira laughed. "Let's go food porn."

"Okay sounds good, text me the details."

"I will, and, Lacey? Just, just so you know, I'm team Lunner."

Lacey laughed and shook her head. "Have you been drinking, Taamira?"

"No silly, I don't drink. I mean I'm team Gunner and Lacey."

"There are teams?"

"Well kind of, most seem to be team Lunner actually."

"What is the alternative?"

"Alternative?"

"To Lunner?"

"Oh, that. Well, there isn't really one. It's just those that are for and against.".

Lacey couldn't believe her ears.

"Who is against us?"

"I don't want to say in case you get mad.".

"I won't get mad. Now, tell me."

"Fine. Astrid thinks you're crazy if you take him on, and so does Mustique."

Lacey's heart was beating ten to the dozen now. "Did they say why?"

"Just that they thought he was too broken. I don't think that. I think you two are perfect for each other, but you know Astrid, she isn't really a commitment person."

"He isn't broken, he's just a little banged up." Lacey realised she believed that in her heart.

"Exactly, and God knows he has reason to be after what he has been through. Liam was so angry when this first happened, but now he feels bad for not being the friend he should have been."

Lacey steered the conversation away from Gunner, wanting to make up her own mind about what he told her later and not be persuaded by well-meaning friends. She wanted him, loved him there was no doubt about that, but was it enough?

Noticing it was now dark, she realised she'd lost track of time and it was nearing eight. Her phone dinged, and she saw a text from Gunner saying he'd be an hour late and asking if that was okay.

She texted back saying it was and then settled to watch *The Crown* on television. Thirty minutes later, she heard the screech of tyres and sat up quickly. Lacey heard shouting and then saw a flash of light as a window smashed in her living room, and a bottle exploded into flames, everything catching on fire around her within seconds.

Lacey stumbled to her feet when another bottle came from the other side and exploded, knocking her back into the coffee table where she hit her head. The pain made her vision blur as smoke began to engulf the room, and then gunshots echoed around her. Coughing, she tried to move forward but was frightened in case she got hit by a stray bullet. Liam was on duty with Waggs tonight, and she knew they had their hands full outside. She had to get herself out of this one.

Crawling with tears and blood dripping down her face, she headed for the door, not caring about the glass cutting into her palms or knees. The smoke would kill her before the cuts, or the fire would.

Holding her arm in front of her face, she tried to take a breath as flames licked up her living room curtains and spreading so fast it made her head spin. Bumping into something she cried when she realised that in the dark she'd gone in a full circle and was back near the table rather than being closer to the door. Dizziness hit her, and Lacey realised that she was completely disoriented.

Blackness began to close in, and she knew that without help, she wasn't getting out of there alive.

Chapter 18

Gunner arrived back at Eidolon around seven-thirty. He hadn't wanted to come in, but the information Bás had given him needed to be passed on to the team so they could make a clear plan of how to proceed. Shooting a quick text to Lacey asking if he could come by later, he felt terrible for messing her around. After all, she was giving him a chance nobody else had.

Her instant reply made him smile, and the tension in his shoulders eased. Walking into the gym, he saw Blake, and not wanting to get into things with him turned on his heel and started to walk away. He hadn't seen Blake since the incident a week ago, and that suited him fine. Jack had called and made it clear that as far as he was concerned his place on the team was still there for him.

Gunner wasn't so sure. Eidolon ran so well because they were like family. They fought, but the trust that nobody could break was there. He no longer had that, and what was more, he didn't feel it either—at least not from Blake. He understood it, but until they cleared that up, he'd left making a decision about his future on hold.

Blake had reached out to him, but he'd let it go to voicemail not wanting to engage when he felt so raw himself. He knew Blake had been looking for him too but wasn't ready to face him. Alex had finally found him in the Litch, drunk off his ass and gotten him a hotel room to sober up in. Gunner was still staying there now although he'd never admit it.

"Gunner, wait up." He wanted to ignore the plea from his former friend, but he owed him this at least. Gunner didn't really blame Blake, had this been Lacey he would have lost his mind. Stopping he waited for Blake to jog up to him. He had his kitbag over his shoulder and had obviously been using the gym earlier. "I don't have a lot of time."

"I understand. I just wanted to say how sorry I was for my behaviour. I still struggle with what happened to her and knowing I wasn't there. It's no excuse but for what it's worth, I know you couldn't have made a different choice. I have sisters, and there is nothing I wouldn't do for them. It was an impossible situation, and I only wish we could go back and we'd known about her."

Gunner wanted to stay mad but in the face of such a genuine apology, he couldn't. He looked away and blew out a breath. "Look I get it. I do, and honestly, I would be the same. I don't care that you lashed out at me, I'm fair game, but Lacey isn't."

"Understood. We good?"

Blake held his hand out, and Gunner looked at it before taking the peace offering. What Blake said was right; he'd allowed this to happen by withholding Milla's existence from his friends. Had they known, this wouldn't have happened. He could've put proper safety protocols in place like the other men had for those they loved.

Gunner took Blake's hand, a weight lifting as he shook it. "We're good."

"Thank God. The couch is getting old really quickly."

Gunner's eyebrows disappeared into his hairline. "Pax still mad?"

"You wouldn't believe it. Grace can hold a snit better than anyone I know."

"A snit? Don't let her hear you call it that or that couch could become permanent."

"Yeah, good point."

Gunner laughed as they walked into the hallway and then they heard a commotion from the war room and both men were running as the sound of gunfire came over the comms. Rounding the corner, he saw Lopez and Decker at the terminal, but it was the sound of Waggs' voice coming through that made his blood run cold.

"We're pinned down by gunfire and can't get to the house. We need back up, stat. The house is burning, and Lacey is inside."

Before the last word was out, Gunner was moving without thought, his only instinct to get to the woman who meant more than anything to him and was inside a burning building. His gut clenched as he jumped in the hummer used for tactical situations. He was about to gun the engine when the door opened and Blake jumped in with weapons and an oxygen breather.

"Thought we might need these." Gunner was glad to have someone thinking with a clear head. The entire journey took less than eight minutes, but it was the longest eight minutes of his life.

He could hear the updates coming through from Liam and Waggs and was relieved when they said the gunmen had left, driving off and leaving two of their men stranded. Gunner knew Waggs would go for the house and try to save Lacey.

His breath caught in his throat when he saw the haze of orange in the sky as he drove towards her house. The sounds of fire engines and emergency vehicles in the distance hardly reached his consciousness as he pulled the car to a stop and saw Waggs walking out of the front door covered in soot and dirt with a lifeless Lacey in his arms.

Gunner felt his heart fall through a hole in his chest as he raced to her, gently taking her from Waggs as Blake helped get Waggs to the ground where he began to cough up a lung. Lacey was covered in blood and dirt, but she had a pulse. Blake turned and placed the oxygen mask over Lacey's mouth, watching her colour and checking her pulse with his fingers against her neck. The steady thump of her pulse reassured him that she was okay, but she'd inhaled a lot of smoke.

Fire crew and paramedics arrived and took over giving her oxygen as they got her onto a gurney and transported her to the ambulance. Gunner didn't let go of her hand, not wanting her to wake up alone and afraid.

The chaos around him dulled, his only focus Lacey. "Come on, Cosmo, wake up and show me those pretty eyes."

Jack arrived on the scene and walked over to him. "She okay?"

Gunner looked to the paramedic seeking reassurance.

"She will be. Looks like she hit her head, so she'll need a CT scan and an MRI to check her out and maybe a day or so to clear her lungs. But we'll know more when we get her to the hospital and she wakes up."

"Keep me updated." Gunner nodded as Jack walked away to take charge of the tricky situation involving his men.

Lacey began to move as the ambulance drove toward the hospital, fighting the oxygen mask on her face.

"Cosmo, keep it on. You need the oxygen in your lungs to clear the smoke." She looked at him as she coughed, and he held her hand tight, letting her know he wasn't going anywhere.

Slumping back against the trolley, she closed her eyes, but this time he knew she was exhausted, not unconscious. Tonight, she'd gotten incredibly lucky. He shuddered to think what would have happened if Waggs and Liam hadn't been there. From now on though he would make sure she was safe. He hadn't wanted to take her out of her home, but this changed everything. He wanted her where nobody knew how to find her, not Osbourne and certainly not Carmine Russo.

Digging out his phone, he sent a text to Jack and then held on tight to Lacey. He didn't care if it took him the rest of his life, he wasn't leaving her alone, and he'd do whatever it took to keep her safe.

At the hospital, they left him to give her details to the desk while the doctors rushed Lacey through. He went to follow and was held back by a formidable-looking receptionist.

"Sir, you can't go back there."

Gunner turned ready to argue and saw Kanan rushing through the door. "Jack sent me, wanted me to make sure you weren't alone."

Gunner just nodded, more moved by the caring than he could say. "Thanks."

"Roz called the girls and Skye is on her way. We'll find the pricks who did this, Gunner."

Gunner knew Kanan well, having worked and socialised with him on many occasions and was glad for the ex-spy's back up.

"Excuse me, sir, does your girlfriend have an allergy?" Gunner felt lost, not knowing for sure if she did or not. He was coming to realise just how little he knew about the woman he loved. As he was about to admit he didn't know, Skye rushed through the door and looked around frantically before she ran over to him when she saw him.

"Does Lacey have any allergies?" Skye gripped his hand and proceeded to answer the questions put to them, by the medical receptionist on duty.

Before long, the waiting room was full of people he knew. Lizzie and Smithy, Lucy and Jace, Zack and Ava, Evelyn, Taamira, Callie, Astrid, Bebe, and Pax. It was overwhelming in a good way to know she had so many people who cared about her.

He sat, his leg bouncing up and down with impatience as he waited for an update. He felt someone sit down next to him and sat straight, his gut clenching when he saw it was Pax.

"She'll be okay, you know. Lacey is tough and won't let a little thing like smoke bring her down."

Gunner looked across at the woman he'd watched get hurt and saw only compassion and kindness.

"I'm sorry, Pax. I'm so damn sorry for what I allowed to happen."

Pax cocked her head. "I won't say I forgive you because there's nothing to forgive. You didn't do it, Gunner. You were a victim as much as I was. You were protecting your sister, and that is noble no matter what you believe about yourself." Pax looped her arm through his and laid her head on his shoulder.

Gunner swallowed around the lump in his throat and nodded not trusting himself to speak for a minute.

"You're a good woman, Grace."

She looked up and grinned. "I know, right! Now to see if I can forgive Blake his idiocy."

Gunner chuckled at a time when he never thought it possible. "He apologised and explained, and we're good now. I know he has my back and I have his and yours."

"Fair enough. It was getting lonely in bed alone."

Gunner patted Pax's hand before a doctor called his name from the double doors that Lacey had disappeared behind.

"Gunner Ramberg!"

He stood and rushed forward with Skye and Nate. "That's me."

The doctor looked around the waiting room with a frown and then looked at him. "Miss Cannon is asking for you. You can go on back when she comes back from her CT scan."

"Is she okay?"

"Yes, I believe so from everything I've seen. I just want to check her lungs and her head and then she can go up to a ward overnight."

"Thank you, doc."

"You're welcome." The man spun on his heel and strode away. He may not have had the best bedside manner, but he'd said all the things Gunner needed to hear, and that was enough.

Gunner went back when Skye nodded and saw Lacey in the bed sleeping. Her hair was messed, her skin was covered in smoke, and she'd never been more beautiful.

He took her hand and brought it to his face, cradling it against his skin as he kissed her palm.

"Hey."

Her gorgeous blue eyes were staring into his. "Hey, Cosmo, how you feeling?"

"Like I have the worst hangover in the world and swallowed a smoking pipe."

"Yeah, that makes sense."

The curtain swept back, and the same doctor from before faced them. "Miss Cannon, your scans are clear. We just want to keep you overnight to make sure your lungs are clear and dress the cuts on your hands and feet. You can go home tomorrow."

Gunner watched Lacey bite her lip and tears fill her eyes. "Thank you, doctor."

The man looked at him and then Lacey and then turned on his heel and left.

Gunner reached out and swept her hair away. "Why the tears?"

"My home."

She didn't need to say more because Gunner knew full well what she was asking. He kissed her forehead and wrapped an arm around her as she leaned into his embrace with a trust that humbled him.

"I'll get an update from Jack as soon as I can, but, Lacey, regardless of what happened with your house, you can't go back there until it's safe. No matter what happens with us, I care about you too much to let you be in danger."

"Where will I go? I could ask Skye and Nate, I guess." She tried to sit up as if she was going to get out of the bed that second and go and fix things, but he placed a firm hand on her shoulder. "Stay there. I'll sort it all out for you if you'll let me?"

He knew he was asking her to trust him even more than she was already and given everything and the fact he still hadn't explained what happened with Pax, it was a big ask.

"Would you? That would be a big help. I feel so tired."

Gunner kissed her hand where the doctor had bandaged from the cuts. "Sleep baby, I won't leave you alone, I promise."

109

Chapter 19

When Lacey woke up from a very fitful sleep, she saw Jack in the corner of her room. He was reading something on his phone and frowning, but he must have felt her eyes on him because he looked up.

"Morning. How do you feel?"

Lacey tested out moving her head, and apart from a slight headache and a sore throat, she felt okay. "Morning, Jack, and okay, I think."

"Good. Gunner had to pop out and sort out living arrangements. He should be back shortly."

Lacey blushed that Jack had read her mind so easily.

"Sorry, I appreciate you being here, I just..." She let the sentence hang because she honestly did not know how to finish it.

"It's fine, Lacey, I get it. Gunner is the one person you want to see when you wake up. He's a good guy." Jack looked away and then back at her. "I'm just sorry it took me so long to remember it."

"It all worked out in the end, though right? I mean he's safe now. You do have his back?" Lacey didn't really have the energy to take on Jack in a verbal sparring match, but she felt bad for how everyone, including herself, had treated him.

Jack smirked. "Yes, Eidolon fully has his back, and bridges have started the process of healing. What about you? Have you forgiven him for Pax?"

Lacey inspected her fingernails as she considered that Gunner hadn't exactly told her anything but on reflection, if Pax could forgive it and now so had Blake, then there was obviously more to the story than she knew. Acting rashly was not like her, but it had been an emotional response. "I think that's between Gunner and me."

"Fair point."

Jack stood and moved toward her. "Your house is salvageable. The fire brigade managed to contain it to the ground floor mostly, but it's going to take a lot of work and will most likely be months before you can move back in there."

"Just as well I was going to redecorate. Do we know who did it, and was anyone else hurt?"

"Everyone is fine, and we're still making inquiries."

The door opened, and her face fell when she saw a nurse instead of Gunner.

"Miss Cannon, let's change those dressings and get you home, shall we?"

Jack moved to the door. "I'll wait outside."

The nurse began to unwrap her hands, and Lacey let her mind go back over last night. She'd been lucky to get out of the house alive, and she needed to thank Waggs for saving her. She remembered Gunner being there in the ambulance and wondered how he got there so quickly.

Fifteen minutes later, with small coverings over the more significant cuts on her hands that had stitches and a prescription for pain relief and antibiotics, she was given her discharge letter. Alone in the room, she was contemplating calling Skye when Gunner walked in. He'd recently showered if his wet hair was any indication and had changed into cargo trousers and a black tee that fit perfectly over his broad, sculpted chest. He had a carrier bag in his hand which looked odd with his overall appearance of manliness.

"Morning, Cosmo." He strode toward her and kissed her head with a smile on his face. "Ready to get out of here?"

"Yes, please."

He placed the bag on the bed and pulled out joggers, sequin slippers, a long sleeve tee, a mini wash kit, and hairbrush still in its packaging.

"I wasn't sure what you would need but thought if I brought the basics you can go crazy online when we get home and get you settled."

Lacey smiled and leaned her head back to look at him. "You're too sweet to me."

Gunner raised his eyebrows and grinned. "Is that even possible?"

"I mean it, Gunner. After the way I was with you, and you still show up when I need you."

He faced her fully as she sat on the edge of the bed, her feet dangling. Lifting a hand, he tucked a wayward strand of hair behind her ear and caressed her face, making her lean into his touch. The scent of his deodorant and the shower gel he used surrounded her, and she felt her belly flutter with desire for him. This was what home smelled like—Gunner was her safety, her happiness, and the only place she wanted to be was with him.

"I have some things we need to talk about when we get home, and we'll talk about Pax too, but let's get one thing clear right now. I'll always show up for you when you need me, and even when you don't, until the day you tell me to stop. I realised this last week that I should've fought harder to explain things to you, to fight for what we were building. I love you, Lacey. Maybe I shouldn't say that or even feel it yet but it's the truth. I'm head over heels for you."

Lacey went to speak, and he held his finger over her lips. "No, don't say anything. Let me tell you what I need to when we get back and then you can tell me whatever is on your mind. It won't change how I feel either way, and I want you to have all the facts first."

Lacey knew this was important to him, but in her heart, she knew the truth already. She loved him too, and she wouldn't change her mind this time or freak out and run. Her heart did a happy flip as it registered the fact he'd said he loved her. She itched to say it back, but she would respect his wishes and only say it when she was absolutely certain.

"How about I get changed, and we can have that chat?"

Gunner lowered his head, giving her time to pull away, but he needn't have worried. She wanted this kiss more than her next breath. She could taste the mint on his lips as the firm, soft mouth touched her own. It was sweet and sexy, and as he pulled away, not enough to convey everything she felt. She swayed into him from the simmering passion and the undiluted passion.

His thumb rubbed over her bottom lip, and he groaned. "So fucking sweet, Cosmo."

He helped her hop off the bed, and she gingerly walked on her hurt feet to the bathroom, with his arm supporting her the entire time.

"Can you manage?"

Lacey cocked her head. "And if I can't?"

Gunner looked down, and she followed his eyes, gasping at the erection outlined in his trouser.

"Oh!"

"Not like it will make me any hornier, will it?"

"Is that a challenge, Mr Ramberg?"

Lacey felt lighter than she had all week, flirting with Gunner despite the fact she'd almost died, and her house was a fiery wreck.

Gunner swatted her ass. "Go before I decide to give the nurses a show they won't forget."

Lacey closed the door on him with a giggle and slowly changed into her new clothes from the hospital gown she'd slept in last night.

After insisting she sit in a wheelchair or he would carry her, Lacey had given in and allowed him to push her to the car and help her inside before buckling her in. The slippers had been perfect for her feet, and she loved the glamour of them, wondering if they were something she could work into her range for teens.

Gunner turned right out of the hospital, but instead of going toward her home, he carried on straight out of the city and headed towards where the Eidolon offices were.

"Are we going to Eidolon?"

Gunner glanced at her. "No. I rented a place from Zack. He has a couple of properties he's been renting out, and this one happened to be available."

"Oh, that's handy."

"Yeah, he saved me a lot of time doing this."

Lacey watched the world go by enjoying the mid-morning sun. "Jack says my house is still standing but has a lot of damage."

Gunner pursed his lips and grabbed her hand, his silent support and acknowledgement holding her steady as reality began to set in.

They passed the turn for Eidolon, and she was surprised when they turned left not far after and onto what looked like farmland. Intrigued she turned to Gunner, who was smiling as he pulled up outside a black and white barn conversion.

"Is this it? It's beautiful."

Gunner looked back at the property and nodded. "Yes, it is. It's an attached four-bed, but Kanan and Roz bought the other one so we won't have any issues."

"Wow, she didn't mention moving to a new house when I saw her."

"Yeah, well, she was too busy orchestrating an ambush."

Lacey laughed. "Yes, not very subtle is she but it's nice to know she cares."

"If you say so."

Gunner helped her inside by lifting her into his arms and carrying her and she wanted to say she minded, but the truth was there was nowhere else she'd rather be. He set her on the sofa, went back outside and brought her bag of pain pills.

"When you feel better, and your pain relief kicks in, I can show you around but let me sort out some lunch first, so it doesn't upset your tummy."

"Sounds perfect. My feet are throbbing."

Gunner lifted her legs and propped them on the couch and then handed her a new phone and MacBook. "The phone is new, but has your number transferred over. The Mac is the one from your office. Luckily that part of the house escaped the fire damage."

"Wow, thanks."

While Gunner made them a lunch of beef sandwiches which he cut small for her hands and some fruit, Lacey got on the phone to her insurance company and got the ball rolling about the house. Her pain pill kicked in, and she felt more comfortable but still tired.

Gunner had kept his distance since they got home, but with the plates cleared away, he lifted her feet as he sat on the other end of the couch.

"I need to tell you some things."

"Okay."

"The first one is something I don't want to tell you, but I promised I wouldn't keep anything from you again, so here goes."

Lacey braced, knowing by his demeanour that she wasn't going to like what he said next.

"I heard from Will that Carmine Russo got early parole."

Lacey tasted bile in her mouth as the food she'd eaten tried to make a reappearance, and her heart began a terrifying gallop.

"No!"

She was in Gunner's lap in the next second, his arms holding her safe against his chest.

"Lacey, I won't let him get to you."

Lacey shook her head as all her hard-won confidence fled, leaving the fearful shell from before.

"You don't understand. He had contacts and he knows people, bad people."

Gunner cupped her cheeks and made her look at him, his blue eyes clear and fierce. "Listen to me, Cosmo. I know people too, and they're the best people. Last time you didn't have Eidolon or Zenobi watching your back but this time you do, and you have me. I won't let him hurt you, do you hear me?"

Lacey nodded, but she was still frightened that maybe Carmine was more cunning than Eidolon or Zenobi.

"I can tell I've got some work to do convincing you but trust me, Lacey. You're safe here. He won't even know where you are as this place is untraceable, Will has seen to that."

Lacey tried to force her stomach muscles to relax and snuggled into Gunner.

"Tell me about Pax."

"One night I got a call from the man I was working for, or rather, being blackmailed by. They had Milla as you already know, but I was pushing back against the things they wanted me to do."

"Like what?"

"They wanted me to sabotage missions so that the Eidolon members got hurt, but I couldn't do it and kept sabotaging the sabotage and making sure Eidolon got information to get them out of the shit in time. I was sent to the Zenobi Gallery and told to wait for a text. Pax was there alone, and I had a heavyweight of dread in my gut."

Lacey felt Gunner squeeze her tight, and she wrapped her arms around his neck, trying to offer him comfort.

"Anyway, I saw two men arrive and go in and followed. I was about to intervene when I got a text. It was a video of Milla in her bed and a man was standing beside her with a gun, his belt and zipper were undone, and I knew…" He shook his head, and she knew this was painful for him.

"The next text said if I interfered in what was about to happen to Pax, then the man would rape and torture Milla."

"Oh, Gunner."

"I know I should've found a way, but at the time I didn't know what to do to save them both, so I saved my sister from something which would've terrified her. She's been through enough already. I couldn't let that happen to her."

"Nobody should blame you for that. Any brother would've done the same thing."

"I still see the men beating Pax in my sleep and it haunts me. Watching and doing nothing while a woman my friend cared about got hurt was the hardest thing I've ever done."

"I'm so sorry I blamed you. You've been shoved into untenable positions and done your best to keep everyone safe with no thanks and no support. You're a good man, Gunner Ramberg, and I truly hope you can forgive me because I love the bones of you. Every single part of you has won over my heart and it belongs to you now."

Lacey saw the doubt followed by the hope flitter over his features and hated that he felt so alone that he couldn't believe himself worthy of love. She vowed to protect this man's heart from any further pain. He may be her protector physically, but she would stand between anyone who wanted to cause him pain.

"I love you, Lacey Cannon, and thank God every day that I met you."

"Ditto. Now, how about you show me the bedroom? I'm feeling sleepy?"

Her arms around his neck, she felt the sexy smile against her lips as he stood and did just that.

Chapter 20

Gunner was surprised to have got a call from Jack early this morning. He'd been lying awake in bed with Lacey draped over him like a blanket, her naked flesh making his body ache to be inside her again. It had been three days since the fire that almost took her from him, and he knew it would be a long time before he got the picture of her unconscious body out of his head.

They'd made love, and he'd shown her with his touch and his body how much he cherished her loving him and what she meant to him. He wasn't sure he'd ever have the words to make her understand just how she'd saved him.

He'd gone from a man almost begging for death, so tired with the world, to one who woke up every morning feeling blessed beyond what he could comprehend.

His phone had vibrated on the nightstand, and he'd seen it was Jack wanting him to meet him an Eidolon. Slipping from the bed and leaving Lacey spread out like a feast was hard but making her safe was more important than anything.

Dressing quickly, he'd sent a text to Kanan next door and told him Lacey was alone and he had to go out for a meeting with Jack and would be back as soon as he could. He'd no intention of stealing into the new father's time with his wife and family if he could help it.

He wrote a note to Lacey and left it by the bed and then filled the kettle for her and laid out her favourite tea mug. He got a text back from K, saying Roz was sending one of her girls over and he relaxed even more.

Gunner locked the door and sat in his vehicle until he saw Bebe, drive into the spot beside him and give him a jaunty salute. He lifted his chin in greeting and pulled out, glad that he was only a few minutes down the road now, instead of miles away. This place had been a godsend, and he was very tempted to make Zack an offer on the place.

Lacey hadn't said much, but he got the feeling she wasn't all that keen on going back to her old place. Which was a shame because it was a wonderful home, and perhaps when it was gutted and decorated, she would feel differently.

They hadn't discussed the future, but he knew for a fact his lay with her, he just hoped she felt the same when all this was over, and she didn't decide he was more hassle than he was worth.

Jack's black Audi Q8 was parked in his spot, and so was Lopez's Ford and Decker's Ducati Black Star. Gunner left the Volvo he'd been driving beside Jack's car and entered the building. It was barely seven in the morning, but he could already feel the hum of life from the place—familiar smells of cooking mixed with the sweat from the gym and the cleaning solution.

It was almost surreal to be there and the feeling of belonging restored to his psyche. So many times he would've done anything to be back here, and now he was, he knew why it'd had such an impact on him.

He headed to Jack's office and knocked on the open door, seeing Decker seated in front of the desk and Jack behind it.

Jack sat forward and Decker turned toward him. "Gunner, come in and take a seat."

"Everything okay?"

Jack nodded. "Yes, we just wanted to run something by you and see how you felt about it."

Gunner rested his arms on the arms of the chair and leaned back. "Yeah, what's that?"

"Well, as you know, Lopez connected the men from the attack on Lacey to Carmine Russo, but I confirmed Osbourne signed the papers for his release. Has he contacted you at all?"

"Bás has, says Osbourne is impatient to get his hands on the details of the tour. I think I've probably strung him out as long as I can now."

"Okay, that works into our plan."

"Your plan?"

"Yes, I have a meeting with the Queen and James Fitzgerald in two days. I want to meet her away from Buckingham Palace. There are too many eyes and ears there but I want you to be with me for the meeting as well as Decker and Blake. Afterwards, I'm going to have James leak it so it gets back to Osbourne that you were there."

"He'll think you trust me completely again, so when I give him the tour, he won't question it."

"Exactly." Decker looked at Jack and then back to Gunner with a cunning smile. The man was a shark in a suit, and probably more deadly than anyone else. He may not be the quickest on the assault course, although he was probably faster than most Marines, but he could get in your head and have you turning a gun on yourself before you'd even realised what he'd done.

"What's the plan for Osbourne?"

"That's what we're going to meet with HRH about. This is something she needs to make the call on, but I'm going to suggest she eliminates the threat at the source and brings in a new Deputy Director and cleans house of all the men Osbourne put in place."

"I think that's the only way to ensure her safety."

Gunner didn't want to ask, but he knew things unsaid did more harm than those spoken of. "What about your father?"

"As soon as I have the evidence I need, he'll be arrested and charged with treason among other things."

"I'm sorry, Jack. That's tough."

Jack shrugged, but Gunner knew it cost him. "What he did to you was worse. Talking of which, how's Milla getting on?"

"I haven't seen her, but from what I understand from Waggs, she's doing well."

"Haven't you been to see her yet?"

"I haven't had a chance yet with everything."

"You should go and take Lacey before it gets so big you can't get over it." Decker was right, he knew that but seeing his sister was always hard, and since the rescue, it had been worse. Seeing his grandmother almost gutted him.

"Yeah, I'll think about it." Decker stood and clapped him on the shoulder.

"The things we avoid only become more powerful with time and avoidance, Viking."

Gunner remained silent but watched him go. "You reckon he ever takes his own advice?"

Jack was watching where Decker had gone. "I think his demons make ours look like child's play, and that's why he keeps them locked away so tight."

"Hmm, maybe."

"So, you down with this plan?"

Gunner assessed Jack and considered the plan. Osbourne was more likely to buy it if he'd been accepted completely.

"His men are still watching me, or at least they were before I whisked Lacey into hiding. They know I was in and out of here a lot and Bás is playing his part too, so yeah, I think it is a good plan. Do you think the Queen will have us pull the trigger?"

"It's what we do, so most likely. She isn't afraid to do what's needed to ensure the safety of the Crown."

"True. Then, yes, I think it will work. Where are you thinking for the meet?"

"Blake is coming in shortly so we can iron that out. Can you stick around for that?"

"Yeah, Bebe is with Lacey, but I left her sleeping."

Jack sat back and rested his hands on his belly. "Things good between you two now?"

One thing about Jack he may be a perpetual bachelor, but he cared about his men and their happiness. "Yeah, they are. Better than good actually."

Jack cocked his head, a smirk on his face. "Am I hearing wedding bells?"

Gunner chuckled. "Maybe but not yet."

"Fucking hell, I'm gonna look like a penguin if you assholes keep making me wear the suit."

"Might be you one day, Jack."

"No chance. I see what marriage did to my mum. I'd never risk pushing this life on some poor unsuspecting woman."

"Best find a suspecting one then, boss man."

"Yeah, like those are everywhere I look. What I need is a strong independent woman who is also willing to accept my job comes first."

"Yeah, good luck with that."

"All joking aside, I'm glad things are working with you and Lacey. I hate the shit that happened to you and that we didn't know about Milla so we could protect you. Will beat himself up over that failing on his part."

"I should've been honest, but it was good old-fashioned pride that brought me low. If I'd admitted what happened with my sister, then it wouldn't have happened, but I was ashamed for my part in what happened to her and hid her away. That's on me."

"I guess we all learned some big lessons."

"Yeah, pride comes before a fall. I'm gonna go grab some grub while we wait for Blake. Want anything?"

"Coffee if any is going."

Gunner stood and made it to the door before he turned to Jack, who already had his head buried in paperwork. "For the record, when you find the right one, she'll never come in second to anything, not work, not your men, nothing at all. She'll consume your every waking and sleeping thought."

Gunner watched as a funny look passed over Jack's face that looked surprisingly like fear before he blanked his expression.

"As I said, this one might be a unicorn."

Gunner laughed and made his way to the kitchen. Finding the coffee grounds, he was making himself toast when Blake walked in with a massive smile on his face.

He walked over to Gunner and slung his arm around his shoulder. "Not sure what you said to Pax, but I'm officially forgiven."

Gunner shrugged his arm off with a grin and buttered his toast. "Not a lot, just the truth. Want some toast?"

"Sure, I need my energy this morning."

"Blake, I do not, repeat do not, want to know."

"Calm down, I never kiss and tell. Especially with the love of my life."

"Thank fuck."

Gunner made them both more toast, and they ate in companionable silence, the tension and anxiety gone between the two men. Once he was done, Gunner took the plates and rinsed them before pouring coffee for Jack.

"Let's get this show on the road."

Gunner and Blake headed for Jack's office, heard him on the phone and stopped. He waved them in and motioned for them to take a seat.

"Love you too, Mum, talk later."

Jack hung up without a shred of embarrassment that they'd caught him telling his mum how much he loved her, and Gunner respected that.

They spent the next hour talking over different options before finally deciding on Sandringham Palace. It would be easier to get her there with minimal fuss, and it was quicker than using Highgrove.

"What about her personal protection officer? Isn't he one of Osbourne's men?" Gunner knew the Deputy Director had penned them in to a degree.

"What if we put a woman into her circle as a lady's maid or lady in waiting?" Gunner suggested, his thoughts going to Zenobi.

"One of Roz's girls?" Jack asked.

"That would work. It means we could still keep the Queen safe and if we allow her PPO to travel with her, we won't need to leak it. Keep it on the down-low as if we want it kept secret, but he plays into our hands."

Jack crossed his arms and scratched his chin. "You think Roz would go for it?"

Gunner pushed the phone across to Jack. "Only one way to find out, boss man."

Jack sighed and picked up his phone. The fact that Roz was on speed dial spoke volumes. When she answered Jack flicked it to speakerphone

. "Hi, Roz. Sorry to bother you when you're just out of the hospital, but I need a favour."

"Ah, Jacky boy, a call from you asking for a favour is practically a gift."

The phone went silent for a few seconds, and Jack looked at them with murderous intent. "Roz, are you still there? You're on speaker."

"Yes, still here. Just savouring the moment."

"Stop being a smartass, Roz. This is about national security."

"Oh well, why didn't you say so? That would have made... absolutely no difference at all."

"Forget it." Jack grabbed the phone to disconnect.

"Wait, wait, calm down. I'm the one with boobs ready to explode and a vagina that looks like a scene from a horror movie."

Gunner looked at Jack with horror on his face as Blake closed his eyes as if trying to rid his mind of that particular image.

"Well, I think you just sorted out birth control for Eidolon for the next twenty years or so," Jack said deadpan.

"Yeah, K is pretty much cured of wanting any more kids, too. Now, what is this favour because I need to go pump?"

Jack held up his hands when Blake mouthed "What?"

"I need to put someone inside the Palace that Osbourne won't suspect, but they need to be close to the Queen to protect her and not an obvious security plant."

"You thinking lady in waiting or lady's maid?"

"Exactly."

"OK, let me give it some thought. I'll help you, but I need to decide who will be best placed for it."

"Thank you, Roz."

"Oh, don't thank me, it's going to cost you."

Jack sighed. "What now? A kidney for the school fete?"

"Ha-ha, no, but the girls' dance school does need new sound equipment and maybe some kit for the circus hoops."

"Fine, send Eidolon the bill."

"Excellent. I'll call you back when I figure out who. Oh, when do you need them and for how long?"

"Day after tomorrow but tomorrow would be better, and not sure how long. It could be short or end up a few months."

"Fine, give me a few."

Roz hung up

"We'll need Lopez to set up a fake history for her and background in case anyone goes checking."

Blake stood. "How about I get him started on that now so that we can get ahead."

Gunner moved to follow. "I'm going to get going."

"Gunner?"

"Yep?" He turned, popping the p as he responded.

"Go see your sister."

Gunner didn't answer, but knew Jack wasn't expecting one either. Maybe he'd see if Lacey would come with him. Somehow everything felt easier with her by his side.

Chapter 21

Lacey stretched and found the bed beside her cold. Rolling she wondered where Gunner had gone, then she saw the note by the bed and smiled.

MEETING WITH JACK.

BACK SOON.

LOVE YOU MILLIONS

Sitting up she saw it was already eight-thirty and threw her legs over the bed, testing her feet as she put them to the floor. She found the pain was still there but not as sharp as yesterday. Flexing her hands, she found the same, except for the cut between her thumb and palm, that still hurt like a bitch.

Moving slowly, she dressed in a pair of white jeans and a pink Bardot top with long floaty sleeves. It wasn't ideal because she couldn't easily do up the jeans with her hands like they were, but it looked cute, and she wanted to look nice for Gunner.

That may not be very forward-thinking, but she didn't care; it was the truth. She'd spent her time with Carmine trying to be a confident woman and had ended up beaten and broken in both spirit and body. With Gunner, the reverse was true, she would happily do what she could to please him because she wanted to, and with every smile her offered her, she became more and more confident.

Finally making it down the stairs in this gorgeous barn conversion with old oak beams and large picture windows, she made her way to the kitchen and smiled when she saw her mug ready to go, just needing hot water.

Looking out of the window, she saw Bebe walking across the courtyard and smiled as she waved. Lacey went to let her in with a smile. "Tea or coffee?"

Bebe hugged her when she came through the door. "Whatever you're making is fine."

Bebe was beautiful, with long thick dark hair, that fell in perfect waves and sloped brown eyes that were flirty and mysterious.

"Looking stunning as always, Bebe."

"I do try, darling, but you know how it is. Even the most gorgeous people have off days."

When Lacey had first met Bebe, she'd found her a little unnerving with her confidence and glamour, and that was coming from a modelling background, but when she'd laughed, Lacey realised she was nothing like that.

Although with her curves, she could make yoga pants a deadly weapon. "How did you draw the short straw?"

Bebe carried the cups through to the living room and set them on the coffee table as Lacey hobbled after her less like a model and more like a ninety-year-old woman.

Bebe snorted. "Believe me this isn't the short straw and I was coming to see Roz about a job anyway. I just diverted here until Gunner gets back."

"I heard you were at the hospital. Thank you."

"Yeah, well, I figured I should after I outed you at the bar that night and you went flying under the bus as you did."

"Ha, I'd forgotten about that. You did kind of out me about me chucking my drinks away."

"So, I guess you're not pregnant then?" Bebe cupped her tea and sat back, looking contemplative.

"No. No baby this time. It's probably for the best, the timing isn't great, and we've only just got together."

"But?"

Lacey looked over her mug at Bebe, surprised the woman was reading her so easily. "I don't know, I guess in some ways I was disappointed. I did cry all over Gunner's shirt, and we weren't even together then."

"You wanted to be pregnant?"

"Yes, in some ways I did. I'm not getting any younger, and I always saw myself as a mother."

Bebe cocked her head. "When I was growing up in India, all my parents talked about was finding me a good husband and having children. I loathed the idea, but now I find myself thinking about having kids all the time. I'm thirty-six next month, and I can't help feeling time is running out for me."

"No man on the horizon?"

Bebe shook her head. "No, and honestly, I'm not sure I'd be a good wife. I'm too stuck in my ways and finicky. I like living on my own. I have Autumn and Mitch close and Waggs too, and that suits me."

"You don't fancy Waggs? He's cute?"

"Waggs is swoon-worthy in every way, but when I look at him, I just see him as a brother and honestly, he's more fucked up than I am."

"Really? He seems, pretty together to me."

"No, he lost his twin and it fucked him up bad."

"Wow, I didn't know that."

"He doesn't talk about it at all but goes home every year on the anniversary."

"That's so sad, and he's such a nice guy."

"Yeah, he is. I wish I did fancy him. Waggs would be an amazing father and husband if he ever let himself get involved."

"So back to you, what will you do with no man?"

"Not sure, maybe go it alone. I've been thinking of using a donor and doing a DIY job."

"That's what I'd do if I found myself running out of time and without a man."

Bebe sat forward. "You would?"

"Absolutely, I'm sure you'd be a great mum."

"I thought there might be some weirdness from people about it."

"Who cares what other people think, and let's be honest, this bunch aren't exactly playing by the rules on anything. My current next-door neighbour is an assassin for freak's sake."

Bebe laughed. "Yeah, news flash, all of Zenobi are. Not the best reference for a mother."

"I disagree, it makes you perfect. Can you imagine any asshole messing with your kid?"

"Well, that's true. I think I might look into it."

"Do it and if you need anyone to hold your hand or the turkey baster, give me a call."

Lacey stood and walked to the kitchen. "I might make some pancakes. Do you fancy some?"

"Sit down, let me make them. Gunner will kick my ass if you get a hangnail, let alone injure your hands any further."

Lacey threw her head back and laughed. "Don't be ridiculous."

Bebe ignored her and began pulling out everything to make the pancakes, so Lacey sat at the island and watched.

"What will you do with your house?"

Lacey frowned and picked at a spot of lint on her jeans. "I'm not sure. That house was meant to be my fresh start, my sanctuary, and now it just reminds me of the place I nearly died."

"So, fix it up and sell it. Cut your losses and find somewhere else with Gunner. I have to say I'd live in a barn with a hunk like that."

"Hey, hands off." Lacey laughed knowing Bebe wasn't interested in Gunner that way in the slightest.

"I'm just saying a house isn't a kid. If it doesn't feel right get rid of it and find a new place. But let me know if you decide to sell it, I might be interested if this other thing works out."

Lacey poured syrup over the pancakes that Bebe pushed toward her and dug in, chewing the delicious fluffy goodness and mulling it over. She loved that house, but Bebe was right—if it no longer felt like home then she should sell it. She knew the only way to know for sure was to go back and see how she felt when a cleaning crew had cleaned the place up.

"I'll give it some thought and let you know."

Bebe waved her hand in the air. "Take your time, I won't need it for a while and honestly, no pressure either way."

The door opened as they finished eating and Gunner walked in, his eyes moving straight to her and moving all over her body to assure himself she was okay before landing on her lips.

"What's all this? I missed out."

He eyed the empty plates with a wink as he stood behind her and wrapping his fist around her ponytail, tugged her head back for a kiss. If she thought about it, she would've been self-conscious, but whenever she was with Gunner, all thoughts left her brain, especially when he kissed her.

"On that very nauseating note, I'll get going and leave you love birds to it."

Lacey blushed as she looked at Bebe who just laughed as she pointed. "I'm so glad my skin is darker and I don't have to worry about shit like that." Lacey placed her cool palms on her heated cheeks.

"Thanks for watching her, Bebe."

"Hey, I'm not a baby."

Gunner slid his arm around her belly. "Oh, I know that, Cosmo."

"Yuck." Bebe made a gagging noise as Gunner walked her out. Lacey started to put the plates in the dishwasher, thinking about how she'd like to take some self-defence lessons. She felt his arms come around her and tilted her head so he had better access to her neck as he rained kisses on her, heating her blood.

Turning in his arms, she clutched his biceps as he held her, with his hands on her ass. "When this is better, will you teach me self-defence?"

"Of course."

"Thanks, Viking."

"My pleasure, Cosmo."

"So, what are our plans today?"

"Well, I had a thought…"

"Oh, yes?"

"Yeah, I thought we could go and visit my sister and my amma? If you don't feel up to it, we can stay home."

Lacey could feel his nerves in the way his arms flexed under her hands. Gunner wanted this almost as much as he didn't. Lacey was touched that he was ready to share this with her already. "I'd love to meet your family, and today is perfect."

Gunner blew out a breath. "Okay then. Let me call ahead and make sure today is a good day and we can go. It's about an hour's drive. Are you sure that's not too much?"

He was nervous, and it made her want to soothe away all his doubts, but she knew these particular demons weren't ones she could slay for him because they weren't about her, they were about something that had happened a long time ago, and it was time he saw the truth.

"It'll be okay, sweetheart."

Gunner didn't answer, but she saw him swallow and dip his head to acknowledge her comment then he made the call.

Chapter 22

Standing on the doorstep of the private, secure home where his grandmother and sister now lived, Gunner felt sick. This was only the second time he'd seen them since the kidnapping, and the first had been more about making sure they were safe and assuring them and himself that they'd stay that way.

This was entirely different. He had the woman he loved holding onto his hand, anchoring him and keeping him from running. He had to expose parts of himself that he hated, the weak, uncertain boy who'd ruined his sister's life.

His feet felt rooted to the spot as if he were physically unable to move as he eyed the door like it was his biggest threat, and in some ways, it was. Once he walked through, he couldn't undo anything Lacey saw or heard. His past would crash wildly with his future, and he prayed at that moment to a God he wasn't sure he believed in that it didn't end with her leaving him.

A tug on his hand made him look down into a stunning smile full of encouragement and love.

"Come on, stop stalling."

Gunner tipped his lips into a smile and gave a small nod, and he walked purposefully to the door and knocked. Seconds later it opened and they were greeted by the guards who ensured the safety of the residence. After checking his identification and going through the protocols Zack and Fortis had put in place to make sure Milla was safe, the security guard admitted them.

He glanced around and noted how warm this building felt, not from the heat, but it felt like a real home, not a hospital. The building was an old estate home that had been refurbished to its former glory but with the added specification for people with special physical and mental needs.

A nurse met him and Lacey at the door with a smile, her clothing relaxed but smart, a pair of slacks giving her an air of professionalism but still keeping the homey feel that she was more of a friend visiting than a medical caregiver.

"Good afternoon, I'm Carol, and I'm Milla's nurse. Would you like to follow me?"

"How is she?" His biggest fear was that she had in some way been hurt and he didn't know it and now lived in her head with the horrors.

Carol looked back over her head with a smile. "Good, she loves the sunroom, and when I told her you were visiting, she got very excited. She sure loves her brother, and it certainly brought a smile to your gran."

"She always loved the sun." He let memories assail him of Milla saying one day she'd live where it was always hot and not in the ice-cold. He'd never cared, loving the cold brutality of the ice and snow. That had lost its appeal after the accident though, and he now preferred a milder climate too.

They rounded a corner and his heart began to kick-up, beating fast as the sickness in his belly made it cramp. He saw his amma first, and emotions flooded him, the tiny woman who now rushed up to him and wrapped her arms around his waist had given up so much, lost so much, and still, she never gave up on either of them. Loving them and guiding them every step of the way.

Gunner let go of Lacey's hand and gently hugged his grandmother to him in a warm embrace. She barely came to his chest, but he could feel the strength in her even now that she was well into her eighties.

"Hey, amma."

"My boy, how I have missed you." She cupped his face and brought him close so she could look him in the eye. Her weathered skin wrinkled but soft against his cheeks and he felt so much love for this woman.

"I missed you too. I'm sorry I haven't come before, I..."

His amma patted his hand. "It is all well, I know you struggle, my son, but you are here now, and you have brought someone for us to meet, I see."

Her eyes turned to Lacey, and he followed her gaze, noting the tears in her eyes, which she didn't bother to hide. He stepped beside Lacey and slid his arm around her, pulling her close. "Amma, this is Lacey, my girlfriend."

"More than a girlfriend I think if I am meeting her." His amma was astute and not one to curb her thoughts.

"Yes, she's everything to me."

130

Lacey leaned into him but put her hand out for his amma to shake. "It is a pleasure to meet you, Mrs Eivinsdóttir."

His grandmother pulled Lacey in for a hug. "Enough with the formality, my grandson loves you then I am amma to you too."

Lacey laughed and returned the hug, and it was beautiful for him to see two women who meant so much to him smiling at one another.

"Yes, amma is perfect and just a little secret, between us," Lacey looked at him as she said it and then back to his amma who was still holding Lacey's arm, "I love him too."

Amma laughed a loud guffaw full of happiness. "How could you not? Look at him. We do not make ugly children in our family and Gunner is a handsome boy."

"That he is."

Gunner felt his cheeks heat and shook his head at the two smiling women. "Stop it, you're embarrassing me."

He looked behind his amma and saw his sister and his heart soured with love. Milla had been a beautiful girl, and as a woman, she was still beautiful. He saw the love in her eyes as he approached the motorised chair she sat in.

He felt his amma and Lacey behind him, but this was about Milla. He'd always tried to treat her like the smart, intelligent woman he knew she was deep inside, locked in a body that no longer did what it was meant to.

"Hi, Milla." He kept his voice soft as he reached her and took hold of her hand, bringing it to his face as he always had. Milla had severely impaired motor functions, and she struggled to do the most basic things like co-ordinating her hands. It had meant many a time he got hit in the face when she was trying to touch him and convey her greeting. Now he did it for her, and he knew she liked that.

"Guuunnner." Her words were said with so much concentration, and tears filled his eyes every time she said his name. It was a lot of work for her, and that she did it showed her love for him.

"I missed you, sis. I'm sorry I haven't been around much lately."

"Thor."

Gunner shook his head, not understanding as he dropped her hand but kept hold of it, wanting her to feel connected to him and him to her. Glancing at his amma, he noticed her and Lacey had linked arms and was watching them closely.

"She loves the superhero films and thinks you're like Thor saving the world." His amma's voice was full of affection.

"Ah, I see." He turned back to his sister and winked. "I'm no superhero, but would you like to meet a real-life supermodel?"

Milla rocked, and he could see the excitement on her face and chuckled. Turning, he held out his hand for Lacey who moved forward slowly and took it, letting him pull her close so he could place his other arm around her back.

"This is Lacey Cannon, and she was a model for Chanel and Dior but more important than that, she's my girlfriend."

Milla began to rock in her chair side to side, and he knew she was trying to communicate but her joy and excitement was hampering her, making it hard for her to control her actions. He was about to intervene when Lacey reached out and took Milla's hand in her own the three of them forming a circle.

"I am so happy to meet you, Milla. Gunner talks about his wonderful big sister all the time."

Gunner saw the happiness on his sister's face and the smile Lacey gave him, and something shifted inside him. A chasm of despair being filled with the love of these incredible ladies who somehow despite his failings, loved him.

His amma had her hands clasped together, and he knew she was treasuring this time, and he should too. "Will you stay for dinner with us, Gunner?"

"Lacey?"

"Goodness, yes, we'd love that. Thank you."

Dinner was a lively affair full of conversation and laughter which he couldn't remember having in a very long time with his family. He'd learned that Waggs often visited to check on the care Milla was getting and on his grandmother and knew he owed his friend more than he'd realised. His guilt and sense of duty toward them had hindered his ability to enjoy his time with them. With Lacey beside him and her zest for life and her love for him filling the gaps, they became a family again.

As he kissed his sister and said goodbye with the promise to come again in a few weeks and genuinely meaning it this time instead of the empty promise it had been before to fulfil a duty, he saw his amma and Lacey talking, their heads close together before they hugged as if they'd known each other for years.

132

Once in the car he waved to his amma and turned to Lacey.

"Well?"

"Oh, Gunner, they're wonderful, and they love you so much, especially Milla. I can't believe how well she gets across what she wants to convey. She is truly amazing and watching you two together is the most profound thing. You have such a beautiful connection."

He kissed her softly, knowing his family watched and didn't care. He was happy, and he wanted the world to know it.

The drive back was filled with hope for the future that he hadn't felt since he was six years old.

Chapter 23

The journey from Hereford to Sandringham had been uneventful. Gunner had managed to catch a few hours' sleep in the car between Jack ranting because he didn't feel Astrid was the right choice for the Queen's lady in waiting and Blake's humming.

He felt lighter since his visit with Milla and his amma, the experience was so positive for him and Lacey. He'd asked what she and his grandmother had talked about, but she wouldn't say, and he didn't want to push it.

Coming up on the Palace he knew that the Queen was already in residence and Astrid was in place. His adrenalin spiked as the car, a bulletproof Land Rover driven by Jack, pulled up around the back of the Palace as if they wanted this visit kept quiet. All three were armed and had special privileges to carry concealed given to them by the Crown.

"Stay alert."

Gunner didn't respond to Jack, but nevertheless, he was on guard as they were met by James Fitzgerald at the service door and led inside. He'd been to Sandringham before and was always surprised by the fact the rooms not used by the Royal Family, but had been converted to offices and quarters, were pretty shabby looking and in need of a coat of paint at the least.

Upstairs was a different matter, opulent and grand; it boasted old wealth and money. Paintings on the walls that were hundreds of years old, vases, silver-gilt gifted by Russian Royalty, furniture, some of it gifts from heads of state or the Commonwealth leaders, and some passed down from monarch to monarch, much like the throne itself.

James walked quickly, like a man who had a thousand things to do, and Gunner suspected he probably did.

"Her Majesty is waiting for you in the drawing-room."

The four men stopped outside the drawing-room doors, and they waited while James knocked and entered, announcing them. When the monarch said for James to send them in, James nodded, and Gunner waited for Blake and Jack to go ahead of him.

The room was stunning with a trompe l'oeil ceiling panel with a golden pheasant painting overlooking the room below. It had cream walls decorated with ornately carved panels and four floor-to-ceiling mirrored doors at the far end. A large log fire burned in the corner where someone had positioned four armchairs around the fire. It was a stunning room, and he could see why Sandringham was a favourite of the Queen.

"Your Majesty." Blake stepped forward and dropped into a bow before he moved forward as she raised her gloved hands, which he took kissed.

"Oh, Blake, how wonderful to see you."

"Ma'am." Jack bowed but did not kiss her hand and nor did she offer. Her relationship with Blake was different, built on a mutual affection from his years as her family's protector. Jack was one of professional respect and affection, which was something entirely different.

"Jack, I do hope we can sort this horrible business."

Her eyes turned to him, and he saw the shrewd head of state assess him as he dropped into a bow.

"Your Majesty."

"Gunner, it is good to see you back in the fold, so to speak."

"It is good to be back."

She crossed her hands and sat, her back straight as a rod and indicated they should too.

"Shall we begin? I have an evening soiree with the Prime Minister, and he is such a terrible bore, but I do like the new lady in waiting you arranged for me, Jack. She is such a hoot, and I must say, very proficient. I should like to keep her when this is done, but I fear that will not happen."

"I'm glad you approve, Ma'am."

"James has explained the issues we are facing, and I have to say I am quite saddened and disgusted that such a man can get into a position of power in this country."

"It is very upsetting, Ma'am."

"What is your suggestion, Jack? You never come to me with problems, only solutions. It is one of the reasons I feel safe with Eidolon."

"Thank you, Ma'am. My suggestion is that Osbourne is taken out of the equation for good and someone else is put in place. We will also eliminate Osbourne's team as a threat and will temporarily put a new team in place until we are sure the monarchy is secure."

"Who would you put in place? Yourselves?"

"No, we thought perhaps Fortis Security could handle it until all the new personal protection officers and the new Deputy Director were vetted and cleared by us."

"Well, that sounds splendid. Are they on board with this?"

"Yes, Ma'am. I spoke with Zack Cunningham last night, and his team is ready to step in whenever we are ready to proceed."

"What of your father, Jack?"

Gunner saw Jack clench his jaw and hated that his friend was being pushed into this position.

"Well, as James knows, my father was behind the blackmail with Gunner, and he will need to be dealt with, but until I have proof, my hands are tied. If you would prefer someone else to take over your protection and security, I would fully understand."

"Good lord no, the sins of the father should not taint the sons. Gosh, if my ancestors judged me, I would be doomed to failure."

Her Majesty cocked her head as she looked at Blake and then back to Jack. "I trust your team, Jack, and you. If I didn't, you would not be here now. It takes courage and backbone to do what you do, and you have saved my life and that of my family more times than I can count in the last five years, ensuring the safety and security of the monarchy in multiple ways. No, you have proved yourself to me, Jack. There is no need to lambast yourself for your father's ill deeds."

The Queen stood, and they followed, as she crossed her hands in front of her in a familiar gesture. "I concur with your plan. See that it is carried out immediately and please keep James abreast of the situation."

Jack dipped his head. "Yes, Ma'am, of course."

Her head turned to Blake. "Do bring Grace next time you visit. I would love to meet her."

"Of course, Ma'am."

Her eyes focused on him and Gunner felt like she could see through to his soul. "Having a family member threatened is a harrowing thing. I am so glad your sister is well, and I understand she is doing well now?"

"Yes, Ma'am, she is doing very well indeed."

"Good. Now you must excuse me, my new lady in waiting is going to show me a few self-defence moves. Isn't that exciting."

Jack went a little pale but inclined his head. "Very."

The Queen motioned for James to escort them out and after bowing one more time, they made their way back toward the car.

"James, keep her here and have Astrid stay close. How many of Osbourne's men are at Sandringham?"

"Two."

"I'll be in touch later but if anything changes at all or if you get a feeling, let me know."

"I will, Jack."

"I should stay." Gunner looked at Blake, who had made the offer.

"I think that's a good idea. You know this place better than we do and can stay close and hidden. I don't like leaving two of the highest-ranking Royals with just Astrid no matter how good she is. If Osbourne gets suspicious, he could strike before we have a chance to end this."

"Agreed." Blake turned to James. "Do you have a secure office I can use to talk with the team?"

"Yes, use mine."

With that settled, the four men went their separate ways. Gunner didn't like the idea of Blake without the team, but he knew Astrid would have his back and all the more because of Pax.

They were in the car on their way back to Hereford and Jack had the entire team patch in on a call while he drove so he could co-ordinate the next part of this very delicate operation. Gunner knew the slightest slip and it would be an international disaster. The fate of the Crown was literally in their hands. His part in this would be crucial, and yet he didn't feel the normal doubt in his ability to do the job well. He just wanted to get it done so he could rid Lacey of the threat Carmine was to her and begin the next chapter of what he hoped would be a beautiful life with the woman he loved.

Thinking of her, he saw a text come through.

LACEY: GOING TO THE HOUSE WITH BEBE TO CHECK OVER THE DAMAGE. TALK LATER. LOVE YOU.

There was nothing wrong with the text, in fact, it was pretty innocuous, yet he had a bad feeling in his gut even though they'd already discussed her going there. He still hadn't found Carmine

Russo and had a feeling Osbourne was helping him. He didn't want Lacey out of the house without him, but he couldn't keep her locked up like a criminal when the real criminal walked free. The best he could do was make sure she had people with her who were experienced with threats and Bebe was one of the best, and he had asked Liam to keep an eye out too.

Questioning of the men they'd caught after the fire had yielded little help, and they'd been passed on to the local authorities through Aubrey. Lacey was as safe as he could make her, and the tracker he'd slipped in her boots ensured he could always find her if the worst were ever to happen. Not that he allowed himself to go there.

As they made it back to Hereford, he shot off another text to her and was relieved to hear she was back home and having a girl's night with the other Eidolon wags as they called themselves. He sent a final text to say it would be a late one and he'd see her later, and then he concentrated all his attention on the job.

Chapter 24

Lacey was feeling a little bit nervous as she put the last tray of almond cookies in the oven. She'd been out with these women on multiple occasions but tonight was different. Now she was dating one of the men, and she felt like she wanted to pass some strange unknown test.

At least Skye was coming too, and even Roz was popping in for an hour which would be fun. Roz was the scariest in some ways, but in other ways, she was the person who broke the ice.

Taamira had called and said given the situation would she be okay with them hosting girl's night at her place and she'd been relieved to say yes. She was still unsure about her house and what she'd do with it but going with Bebe today had been a little heart breaking. Liam being there with Waggs she knew was Gunner's doing, but she'd been glad to have people around her so she didn't fall apart.

Gunner had wanted her to cancel when he found out the loss adjustors visit coincided with his trip to London, but she'd insisted she'd be fine. Lacey had wanted him there, but she would not be a clingy vine of a woman who couldn't function without her man or at least she wouldn't admit it.

The doorbell rang, and Bebe popped her head in the door. "It's only us."

Lacey waved them inside. "Come in, come in."

Skye had Nate drop her off earlier and was just piping gin flavoured cream filling in some raspberry macaroons she'd made.

Evelyn, Pax, Callie, Taamira, and Autumn trooped in with dishes and bottles in their hands. Bebe had Mercy, one of the other Zenobi girls with her, but Lacey didn't know her well.

"Put everything on the island and let's start with a drink shall we." Pax clapped her hand and moved toward the bottles of alcohol, where she proceeded to take drinks orders from everyone. Lacey took the cookies out of the oven and popped them onto a tray to cool. Roz grabbed one, and she slapped her hand.

"Oi."

"What? I'm breastfeeding, I need my energy."

Lacey rolled her eyes. "Fine, but only one."

Roz poked her tongue out at Pax who moaned that was unfair.

They took their drinks and some crisps and dips into the other room and sat in the large living space that overlooked the countryside with fields as far as the eye could see.

"You roll your eyes, Pax, but I kid you not, this kid is sucking the life out of me, and I mean literally."

"Roz, we've all heard your birth story, or should I say horror story, and there are some of us who haven't had that experience yet, and you're scaring the crap out of us." Evelyn glared at her boss who just shrugged and popped the cookie in her mouth.

"Now what I want to know is how it's going with you and Gunner." Evelyn wiggled her eyebrows at Lacey who blushed as all eyes landed on her.

"Seriously Ev, you're not going even to try and be subtle about this?" Callie shook her head and looked heavenward.

"Hush, Callie, we all want to know, so why beat around the bush."

Callie looked at her. "You don't have to answer if you don't want to."

Pax laughed and took a breadstick and dipped it in the homemade bacon and onion dip. "No, of course she doesn't but it will be easier and quicker than Evelyn wheedling it out of her all night."

Lacey laughed and took a swig of her Cosmo to calm her nerves.

"It's going well. I met his sister and grandmother, who are amazing and wonderful."

"You met his family already?" Taamira asked her head snapping straight.

Lacey nodded. "Yep, the day before yesterday actually and they're so nice. We had dinner and talked, and he was so good with his sister. You can tell how much he loves her."

"Yeah, he ain't the only one." Roz grimaced as she took a sip of her alcohol-free cocktail.

"What does that mean?" Lacey crossed her arms.

"Just that we can see how into him you are."

"And is that a problem? Because I'm telling you if it is or it offends you in any way, then you can leave right now. Gunner is a good man dealt a horrible hand in life, and he blamed himself for a long time, and I won't have anyone who isn't fully on his side bad-mouthing him."

The room was silent for a beat, and then Pax took her hand, forcing Lacey to look up. "Lacey nobody in this room is against you, and even those who are wary were only that way because they doubted Gunner could find it in him to care if he lived or died. I don't need to tell you the toll this entire situation has taken on him both physically and mentally. Decker admitted to Blake that he wasn't sure if Gunner would survive it because he'd given up wanting to live. But since he met you all that changed. Gunner is different, he has a purpose and a different outlook. Deck says he's never seen anything like it in all his years of profiling."

"So, you all don't harbour ill-feelings towards him?"

Pax patted her hand. "Of course not, he's a good man, and finally he's beginning to see it for himself."

"Oh, in that case, I'm sorry I overacted."

The rest of the evening was relaxed as everyone ate the delicious calorie-laden food and drank the sugary drinks until Evelyn, Pax, Callie, and Taamira got a text at the same time she did.

Roz and Bebe looked at each other as if by some telepathic link they knew what was happening and she looked down in dread at the text from Gunner.

GUNNER: TAKEDOWN WILL BE TONIGHT. WILL BE GOING RADIO SILENT IN TWO HOURS AND BACK ONLINE AS SOON AS I CAN. STAY WITH ROZ OR BEBE UNTIL THIS IS DONE AND I KNOW YOU ARE SAFE.

LACEY: STAY SAFE AND DON'T WORRY ABOUT ME. LOVE YOU X

GUNNER: LOVE YOU MORE. X

"Well, that put a downer on the night," Pax said with a frown.

"Yes, I hate the thought of Liam in danger."

"This is a big takedown, it's been years in the making and has so many moving parts. A lot could go wrong," Evelyn admitted.

"Nate left for London earlier this evening with the rest of the Fortis Team. They're going to provide security for the Royal Family until they can get something else in place." Lacey grabbed Skye's hand and squeezed. Nobody liked the idea of the men they loved in danger, but the truth was they wouldn't be the men they were without the risk that surrounded them, and those were the men they loved.

"I should get home. K is manning the fort, but I know he'll want to be at Fortis to provide support if they should need it."

Roz stood, and that seemed to be everyone's cue to leave. Lacey kissed and hugged her friends, feeling the tighter bond had been forged tonight and especially in the last few minutes. She didn't know the details only what Gunner had told her might happen, but she knew it was a big job.

"You should come to stay with me tonight. Gunner won't want you alone with that asshole ex of yours on the loose." Roz stood on her doorstep looking every inch the badass she was, her body already losing the soft look of post-pregnancy.

"I will. Let me clean up, and I'll be over in an hour or so. Is that okay?"

"Yes, I'll leave the door open."

"Okay."

Lacey closed and locked the door and sighed. She was tired but tonight had been just what she needed. Looking at the plates on the coffee table she decided to get it all in the dishwasher now, so the food didn't stick. She pottered around thinking about what Gunner and the others faced, not really able to fathom the danger. A flash of headlights lit the kitchen, and she watched as K backed out and drove away to do his bit.

It was strange how this big family had come to be with no less than three different private agencies linked by marriage and friendship, and now they were collaborating to keep the most important woman in the world safe.

Happy that her home was restored to its former order, she went upstairs to grab her toothbrush and pyjamas and shoved them in an overnight bag. Sliding her feet into her comfy Ugg boots, the only ones that felt nice on her delicate feet, she switched off the lights and walked next door to Roz.

The door was open, but she still knocked out of habit. "Hello, Roz?"

Hearing no reply, she went further and closed the door behind her. She didn't call out again for fear of waking the children. The layout was similar to the one next door, so she walked past the entryway and into the living room and seeing nobody, headed for the stairs.

Roz must be feeding Deacon in the nursery, which she'd seen the day after they arrived and was at the end of the hall next to Roz and Kanan's room, although the baby was in with them for the foreseeable future.

Passing Natalia and Katarina's room, she saw the girls were both sleeping and smiled. It was sweet to see them so relaxed and happy after the start they'd had. Hearing a slight noise which sounded like baby's mew, she continued to the nursery and pushed through the door, seeing Roz on the far side of the room on the floor.

Frowning Lacey moved to help her up and jumped as the door closed behind her. Spinning, she saw her worst nightmare. Carmine Russo was holding baby Deacon in his arms and had a wicked-looking gun next to the child's head.

"Hello, beautiful, did you miss me?"

"Carmine, what... what are you doing here?" Lacey was aware that Roz was injured. She had no idea how badly, but she was moving slightly.

"I came for you beautiful. We have unfinished business, remember?"

"Give me the baby, Carmine."

Carmine looked at the child with a glint of evil in his eye, and she wondered how in hell she'd ever thought he was handsome. The malice practically emanated from his black soul.

"What, this baby?" He made a show of dropping Deacon which made the baby cry and she jumped forward to try and catch him. Bile rose in her throat as she tried to keep the terror at bay.

"Just give him to me and we can leave. Go someplace quiet and talk."

"Yes, I want to talk. To make you understand how much you hurt me."

"I'm sorry I hurt you."

He cocked his head. "No, but you will be."

Lacey had never been so frightened in her life, but she had to keep it together, or baby Deacon and Roz would die.

"Here take that rope and tie that bitch up." Lacey did as Carmine instructed, not making the knots as tight as she could, sensing Roz was coming around and would be able to save Deacon at least.

143

"Now put the brat in the crib and walk towards me."

Lacey cradled Deacon close, kissing his downy head and muttering a quick prayer that his crying wouldn't wake the girls. Placing him in the cot, she moved towards Carmine.

He grabbed her hair and hauled her forward, kissing her roughly, biting her lip until she tasted blood and grabbing her breast hard, pinching her nipple.

"Feel that beautiful. You still want me." Lacey was using all her skills to keep from puking on his Italian leather shoes. Carmine lifted his hand, and she saw the gun coming at her head but couldn't stop it as pain exploded in her eye and the world went black.

Chapter 25

It had been a while since Gunner had flown a bird like this one owned by Eidolon, but it felt good to be back as he landed the chopper in a field close to where he was supposed to meet Osbourne. Bás had come through and managed to make sure the key players were in place. The only one that was not one hundred percent was Frederick Granger. Fortis was ready to seize control of Buckingham Palace security. Blake and Astrid had secured the Queen and the King Consort and were waiting for the word to take down her PPOs.

Gunner made sure his mic and comms were secure before checking his weapon one more time. His job was to draw Osbourne out with the promise of the thumb drive and plans, then the rest of Eidolon would move in and take him and his men out. This wasn't a mission where Osbourne would live—he faced death for his crimes with only them as his jurors.

It irked Gunner that the man would still receive all the accolades of his title, but none of this could ever come out. He would die at the hands of a random criminal shooting and be hailed a hero for the work he'd done.

"This is Viking, check."

Mitch's smooth voice came over the radio *"Viking, we have visual on you."*

Knowing that he had these men watching over him made him feel more confident about this takedown. Arriving at the rendezvous point at an abandoned cattle farm on the outskirts of London Gunner waited.

"We have a visual on Wasp," Jack announced, and Gunner felt his heart rate slow, his instincts sharpen, and his brain clear of all the dross and clutter until it was just him and the mission.

"King and Queen are in place to secure. George and Wilma and Fortis are ready for your sign."

Gunner wondered if the Queen knew Eidolon had given her the nickname Wilma on operations or that Astrid and Blake now had King and Queen as their code names. Wasp fit Osbourne perfectly, the man was a pest that had no good in him only evil intent, looking for its next victim.

145

Gunner stepped forward as Osbourne walked into the dim lights of the farmyard covered in shit and hay as the drizzle that had been forecast began to fall.

"Do you have it?" Gunner could practically feel the urgency as the man held out his hand for the weapon he would use to end the Queen's life. They didn't know his exact plans, but he'd made it clear that he wanted power and to have that he needed to control the Crown, and this Queen was not a woman to be controlled by anyone. Gunner suspected it had to do with the mission where Siren had been a target but had no evidence.

"I have it, but I want to know why you want it before I hand it over."

He could hear the go sign as Fortis went into the Palace through the service entrance James had left open for them, followed by the low pop, pop as they secured the security rooms. He waited a beat, hearing the rustle of movement as Fortis moved silently and then a shout and more pops. He waited a moment longer and then Zin came over the line.

"Jester secure."

Gunner knew that meant Fortis had secured the outer rooms and were moving on to the next phase to secure.

He turned back to a blustering Osbourne, his cheeks going puce with anger the hand by his side twitching as if he wanted to pull a gun and kill the man who dared question him. Gunner remained calm, his features showing no emotion, his hands hanging loosely by his sides. He wanted to make sure the Queen and all of the Royals were secure before he finished this.

"What the fuck has that got to do with you? Now is not the time to grow a pair of balls, Ramberg."

"Oh, really, and why is that?"

"Because it is too late, soldier. The monarchy will fall, and the rightful heir will take the seat of power with me at his back."

"And who is the rightful heir?"

Osbourne laughed. "You really have no idea, do you?"

"Approaching residence."

Gunner recognised Jace's voice through the comms. Being Jack's, cousin he'd been at a lot of Eidolon functions, and by that, he meant piss ups. He needed to stall Osbourne until this last part of the

146

mission was completed. It was also the most dangerous as the men close to the Queen could put her in danger if this went wrong.

Gunner breathed through the anger firing his blood and tried to glean more information.

"Why don't you spell it out for a simple soldier, Osbourne?"

"No, I think it's more fun to watch you squirm and especially now that your woman is back in the arms of her ex-lover thanks to Frederick and you're no longer needed."

Every cell in Gunner's body turned to ice at those words, and he reacted on instinct. The plan had been to try and get a confession first in case it ever came out and the Palace needed a reason for his death, but now he just wanted him dead and this over so he could call Lacey.

"Fred and Wilma are secure."

As those words left Zack's lips, Gunner knew the Queen was safe.

"Golden goose."

Before the last syllable left his lips, Osbourne's head exploded, and a series of pops went off around him as men hidden from his sight fell dead to the ground, killed by the men watching over him. Gunner ran straight through the middle of it all as if he was bulletproof, his only thought getting back to Lacey.

He reached the chopper and saw Waggs run from the woods nearby. His job had the most risk, so it made sense for the medic to be close.

Gunner was calling Lacey as he threw on headphones and started the bird. Waggs jumped in beside him and closed the door, taking his own phone out and dialling a number. Gunner could hardly focus on what he was doing, his brain on autopilot as he tried again to reach Lacey and failed.

There could be a perfectly normal explanation for her not answering. It was two in the morning, and she could be in a heavy sleep, but every sense of urgency in him told him this wasn't the case.

They hadn't been able to find Carmine since he'd been released from prison and that wasn't normal, not for a team who had both Will Granger and Lopez on their side.

He could hear through his comms as news came through that the Queen and the King Consort were safe and that Fortis had taken the

Palace. James Fitzgerald would ensure the woman taking over as Deputy Director had all the information she needed, if not all the information.

The press office would handle the news of the accident, and news of the tragic death of Deputy Director Osbourne and any other loose ends would be handled between the agencies of Fortis, Zenobi, Eidolon, and the Palace.

"Viking, I just heard from K, Carmine attacked Roz in her home. He threatened Deacon and Lacey agreed to go if he left the baby alone."

Waggs was watching him closely as he relayed the information and Gunner held a death grip on the chopper's controls, not allowing emotion inside his head. If he did, he'd lose his mind, and he needed to stay in control so he could hunt down Carmine, get Lacey back safely, and then slit the bastard's throat for touching what was his.

"Get Bás on the line." Gunner knew his tone was harsh, but he also knew Waggs would do what was needed.

The night sky seemed to stretch endlessly in front of him as he made his way back towards Hereford, a thirst for blood on his tongue seeking vengeance for every hair he hurt on Lacey's head and that was before he started avenging Deacon.

"Viking, this is Bás."

"What the fuck happened, Bás?"

"Not sure. Last I heard Osbourne didn't know where Russo was."

"What about Frederick Granger?"

"He's with Osbourne, isn't he?"

Gunner looked at Waggs, a moment of understanding passing between them. "No, he fucking isn't."

"I'll find him."

Bás hung up and Gunner fought with whether he'd been a fool to trust the man, but he'd shown him nothing but support.

"Gunner, I have Cosmo on the radar. Her tracker is holding still at her place of residence." Lopez had been lightning-fast off the mark to find her, and he realised every free agent would be looking for her.

"ETA is thirty minutes. Who do we have free?"

"Just Zenobi. K won't leave Roz who's fit to be tied."

Gunner knew that threatening the newborn baby of a woman like Roz was a death sentence and if he weren't feeling so bloodthirsty right now, he'd let her have at it.

"See if Bebe, Evelyn, and whoever else they have available will check it out?"

"On it."

Never had a journey seemed so long, the feeling of helplessness that was overwhelming him was almost so thick he couldn't breathe.

"Stay frosty, Gunner, we'll get her back."

Gunner glanced at the man who had been the quickest to forgive his sins with desperation on his face. "What if he hurts her before I can get to her?"

Waggs pursed his lips, his jaw ticking with anger. "Then you help her heal, brother. We all do."

Waggs nursed his own pain so privately nobody knew how broken he was, but Gunner had seen it. While he'd been working for the enemy, he'd followed Waggs when he'd gone back home to see his parents on the anniversary of his twin brother's death, and Gunner had witnessed his pain first-hand.

He hadn't told a soul and would carry it the grave, but it was that knowledge that made him sure Waggs would do what it took to stop others feeling the same grief that consumed him.

Chapter 26

Lacey woke with a jolt, her heart hammering in her chest as the memory of what happened slammed into her. The smell of stale smoke was the first thing she noticed as her eyes adjusted to the darkness. It took a minute before she realised where she was, the pain in her cheekbone throbbing and clouding out everything else.

Rolling over, she welcomed the softness of the mattress beneath her, but the pull on her shoulders made her realise that someone had bound her wrists and ankles with a soft tie. Lacey tried to sit up, her stomach muscles tensing, and she thanked yoga for her core strength. Swinging her legs off the bed, she realised she was in her own bedroom but not why, and that was the most important question, or perhaps she did know and fear was the thing keeping her from facing it.

A figure moved from the corner, and she bit back the scream in her throat as she saw Carmine move into the light coming through the balcony window cast from the moon. He'd dressed as he always did in a three-piece dark suit, the red tie he usually wore was missing and she knew then what the softness on her skin was. Lacey would have preferred the rough burn of rope or plastic to this pseudo kindness. Black hair swept back from his high forehead, it was difficult to see the handsome man she'd met who had charmed her and made her laugh. Maybe it was the truth of his character that made him seem so hideous to her now.

"I see you're awake, beautiful."

Her pulse pounded in her neck so hard it was almost painful, and she was convinced she was about to have a heart attack from pure fear. It took everything in her not to shy away from him as he moved closer, yet her body still shook. When he stroked her cheek, the impulse to pull away was too strong, and she yanked from his grasp.

Carmine's face twisted in a cruel mask and he grabbed her chin in a painful grip she knew would leave bruises. "Don't you pull away from me! You belong to me, Lacey, and I'll touch you whenever I wish."

Anger surged, and despite the tears on her cheeks, she locked eyes with the man who'd tortured her and hurt her in ways no woman should ever be hurt. A man who was cruel and nothing like the man who now loved her, a man who cherished her and valued her as a person.

"I belong to no man."

Carmine pushed her away and laughed in her face. "Is that what you think, Lacey? That you aren't property?"

He began to pace as she watched him like a hawk, making herself ready should an opportunity arise to save herself. Gunner and the team were away and, *please God*, she prayed Roz was safe, but there was no guarantee anyone would find her in time before whatever Carmine had planned for her happened.

"I'm not property. I'm a person."

"No, you're a trophy, a beautiful trophy, and you're mine."

"What do you want from me, Carmine?"

"Everything, Lacey. I want you to commit, to love me and give me heirs to show my father and brother that I can make you submit to me."

Lacey angled herself until she was facing her tormentor as she wiggled her feet. She needed out of these binds if she had any hope of saving herself, but they were too tight for her to get out of.

"I need to use the bathroom."

"Can't it wait?"

Lacey ignored the petulant response and answered him, playing to his weakness. Carmine found menstrual blood disgusting, and she used that against him. "Not unless you wish to clean up the blood that is about to leak from my body."

His lip curled, and she saw the open disgust on his face. He moved close and pulled her roughly to her feet, untying the silk from her ankles and wrists. It dawned on her that her feet were now bare, and her last shred of hope that the others would find her faded. Her boot with the tracker inside was nowhere in sight, and she was on her own. Carmine stood by the bathroom door that led to a darkened space behind her, the electric still off from the fire.

He grabbed her by her hair and angled her face, so his lips were next to her ear. "Don't do anything stupid, little girl." He shoved her away and stepped back as if her blood could somehow taint him. Lacey wasn't on her period, that problem only lasting a few days, but it was her memory that had served her this time and the way he treated her every month as if she was a leper that needed to be confined to a room with no visitors.

Lacey closed the door and looked around for a way out of her nightmare and found none. Her breathing coming too fast made her dizzy as panic began to overwhelm her. Dropping her head, she braced against the sink and tried to control her breathing. When that was under control and the near-meltdown had passed, she decided to use the bathroom while she had the chance, not knowing when the next opportunity would present itself. Spotting a bottle of talc on the side, a hint of an idea came to her, and she hoped like hell it worked.

Eyeing the talc and trying to visualise the bedroom, she took a breath and readied herself. If this didn't work, she was dead because she wouldn't go with him willingly or allow him to touch her ever again. She'd worked too hard to be free, to see herself as worthy of the love of a man like Gunner.

Her heart broke as she thought of him. He'd blame himself if anything happened to her, his sense of guilt too strong. It was one more reason for her to get herself out of this mess. She wouldn't allow him to go through life as he had; she wanted to be by his side, showing him they both deserved happiness.

Carmine hammered on the door, making her jump. "Hurry it up."

"Just coming." Lacey quickly washed her hands and took a breath as she grabbed the talc and removed the lid. She had one chance at this, and it had to work.

With the lid off and the powder behind her back, she opened the door using the darkness to disguise her intent. Carmine turned to grab her, and she brought her hand forward quickly throwing the fine powder at his face. He screamed, and she ran for the bedside, snatching the lamp and swinging with everything she had. Carmine screamed and went to his knees, but he wasn't out, and she knew she had to run.

Lacey ran for the stairs, her feet slipping on the wood flooring in her haste. Getting to the bottom, she grabbed the handle and realised the front door was locked. She could hear Carmine moving and knew she had seconds to make a choice. Running for the back door and away from the boarded-up windows at the front, she sighed in relief when she saw the keys in the back patio door. Turning the key and flicking the switch she could have cried when the door slid open, the cold night air bathing her skin. Feet on the stairs had her bolting out into the night and towards the woods and the river.

Twigs cut into her bare feet, painfully tearing at the wounds already there. Branches lashed at her arms and face, but she still ran, knowing to stop would mean the end for her. Carmine was behind her, closer now as she heard the running water of the river up ahead. Making a split-second decision, Lacey headed for the water. She couldn't outrun him, but she could definitely outswim him.

Standing on the bank watching the river rush past with only the moon to see, she panicked over what to do but the sound of Carmine moving closer reached her and she knew she was out of time and slipped into the frigid water.

Already up to her waist at the bank, she could feel the current pulling at her legs as she sank lower and began to swim for the other side, knowing Carmine wouldn't follow.

"Lacey, you won't escape me."

Lacey turned and saw him on the bank of the river watching her and then felt horror as he followed her into the water. The water was deep as she reached the middle, and she'd misjudged the impact of the earlier rainfall and how bloated the river was with rushing water.

Her arms began to tire, and her legs ached as she kept swimming, turning just once to see Carmine was in trouble. His body flailing as he tried to fight against the current, but he seemed to be caught on something, and his head kept going under.

"Lacey, help… help me."

He went under again, but Lacey couldn't help him; she was fighting for her own life. Keeping her own feet up so as not to get caught on anything in the river, she turned to swim at a forty-five-degree angle to the current and hoped it helped push her to shore as her body began to tire.

Focusing on that, she didn't see the log coming at her quickly until it hit her, and she went under, the black swirling murk of the water sucking the air from her as it rushed at her so fast she couldn't fight it. Her body was sucked under as her need for oxygen began to overwhelm her.

Black spots tinged her vision, and her lungs burned with pressure to take a breath that would hold nothing but the water that would flood her lungs. As the desperate instinct to breathe won out, she opened her mouth, and the world went black.

153

Chapter 27

Gunner raced past the house towards the woods, his only worry getting to Lacey. Bebe had arrived moments before him and pointed toward the woods. "She ran for the river."

Gunner knew Lacey was a good swimmer and once inside the woods made a split-second decision that could either save her life or cost them both. He had little choice, but to track someone in the woods at night took time and patience he didn't have.

A sense of urgency rode him as he felt Waggs right behind him, covering his six. He heard a man say her name up ahead and knew he was on the right track and picked up speed. His feet eating up the ground beneath him as he pushed harder and faster. He just needed her to hang on and not give up. He was coming, he just prayed to God he was in time.

The trees opened up, and he saw the rushing river in front of him lit by the moon. A sound to his left made him turn, and he saw Carmine Russo in the river fighting to stay above the swollen body of moving water. Looking past that he could make out the blonde hair of the woman he loved about ten metres ahead also fighting the current. His heart skidded to a halt as she turned, and he saw a large fallen tree limb hit her, sending her under.

Without another thought, he rushed into the water and swam as fast as he could, even with his strength finding it hard going against the force of mother nature. He passed Carmine without a shred of guilt as the man continued to be pulled under but not moving downstream, indicating he was stuck. Carmine wasn't his problem. All he cared about was Lacey.

Getting to the spot where she'd been struck by the log, Gunner dove, reaching out into the dark and finding only water. His lungs were fighting for air he swam for the surface taking a giant gulp of oxygen before he dove again, swimming further downstream and sweeping his hands out in an arc and finding dead space.

Twice more he did this, his panic swirling like a massive beast ready to condemn him and then on the third go he felt it, the silk of hair on his fingers. Reaching for it, he dragged her into his arms and

154

swam for the surface. Sucking in a lungful of air, he tipped her to her back and found her body lifeless.

This incident was so similar to the day Milla had been hurt, not in how it happened but the water, the feeling of absolute terror and panic, he could hardly bear it. Waggs met him halfway and helped him drag Lacey to the shore.

Laying her on her back, Waggs began CPR and Gunner held her hand and prayed.

"Come on, Lacey, breathe. Don't you leave me. I can't do this without you, I love you so much, Cosmo. You saved me from the darkness. Don't you dare die on me." He could feel the wetness on his face, not from the river water but the hot tears that flowed from him.

Every second that Waggs worked on her became an hour as he willed her and begged her to come back to him, knowing his life would be over without her in it. She was the one. The person everyone searched for, and he'd never thought he'd find that. She was his miracle, and he wouldn't lose her now.

Memories flooded him of watching the same life-saving manoeuvre being preformed on Milla, and the outcome from that weighed heavy. Like history repeating itself in a cruel and tormenting sequel to the events of the past.

His heart almost stopped when Lacey jerked and coughed, river water spilling from her lips as Waggs turned her onto her side. Gunner felt the knot of fear release as he took in the sound of her coughing and breathing, but he was unsure if she'd been affected by the lack of oxygen.

It made no difference to whether he loved her or not if she was harmed in some way. He'd spend eternity caring for her but as she looked around and her eyes fell on him, and he saw the smile she gave him he knew that his Cosmo was going to be just fine.

Hauling her to him as Waggs moved out of the way he held her tight, not ever wanting to let go.

"I knew you would come."

"I'm so sorry he got to you."

Lacey looked up with determination in her eyes and if he hadn't already been head, over heels for her seeing that look in her eye would have done it. "No, this isn't on you. This is Carmine's doing not yours."

"I love you, Lacey Cannon."

"I love you too, thanks for saving me."

"I didn't save you, you saved yourself."

"Well, not entirely." She cocked her head at the river where Waggs was dragging Carmine's lifeless body onto the bank.

"Is he dead?"

"Yes, Cosmo, he's dead."

He could hear the sounds of people coming toward them and turned, surprised to see Roz walking toward them.

She stopped and looked down at them. "You good, Lacey?"

Lacey nodded in his arms. "Yeah, I am now."

Roz crouched and dipped her head before she looked up at both of them, focusing mostly on Lacey. "You saved my son's life, and for that, I will forever be in your debt. Zenobi is at your service any time you need us, you hear."

"Anyone would have done the same."

"No, they wouldn't have. He got the drop on me but you saved me and the people I love. There are bad people in this world, but you, Lacey, are one of the best."

"You're an exhausted new mother, Roz. Go easy on yourself."

"I should have protected them."

With that, Roz stood, and they watched as she walked toward Carmine's body and looked down on him before bringing back her boot and kicking his lifeless body hard.

"That's for threatening my son and anything else you did. I will see you in hell, asshole."

Then she walked back into the woods and disappeared.

"I am so glad she likes me." Lacey laughed, and he chuckled thinking only minutes before that he'd never smile again.

"How about we get you checked out at the hospital and then go home? I think we deserve a few days off?"

"That sounds like an excellent plan."

At the hospital, they checked Lacey over. It was the same doctor as she'd seen before, and Gunner's calm exterior cracked a little under the strength and fortitude Lacey showed. The police came to take statements, but Aubrey, the detective in charge and Will Granger's fiancée, shooed them away and said she'd come out to the house and take it tomorrow when Lacey had rested.

156

Gunner got word that everything had gone smoothly at the Palace and at Sandringham House and the press office would announce a new Deputy in the morning after the sad news of the recent Deputy's death. Waggs had stayed with them until the doctor had given Lacey the all-clear then he'd left to go back to Eidolon. He would help Lopez find Frederick Granger, who it seemed had disappeared without a trace but not before they'd found out he'd been the one helping and hiding Carmine Russo.

The news that his father had helped Carmine would gut Jack and Gunner knew he'd hunt his father down, and not give up until he found him. Jack was a man with integrity and loyalty, and he'd take this personally because what could be more personal than your own father trying to ruin you.

Gunner vowed to be beside Jack every step of the way, and he knew the others would too. Eidolon had come through for him when it mattered, and he knew nothing would shake the new bonds that had been forged through betrayal and pain.

As before, the hospital waiting room was full of people who loved Lacey and him and he felt so fortunate to have that, but it was the call he received from his amma that brought him to his knees and showed him how loved he truly was.

"We saw on the news that Lacey nearly drowned. Please tell me she is okay."

Of course a woman like Lacey getting hurt would always make the news, and she'd decided to be open about Carmine Russo and what he'd done to her in the hopes that it would help others in her situation feel less alone and maybe find the courage to get away or seek help.

"She is fine. It was close, but she's going to be alright."

"Oh my, Gunner. How awful for you both. It must have been so horrible for you reliving the fear from what happened with Milla."

"I'm fine, Amma."

"I know you say that, but for a lot of years, you were not. I know you blamed yourself, but nobody else did. It was a terrible accident that couldn't have been foreseen. I'm so glad you have Lacey, and she has you. Please give her our love and bring her by to see us soon. We miss you, sweet boy."

"I love you, Amma."

"Oh, I love you too, so much."

When he hung up, Gunner smiled realising that his past no longer had control of his future. He'd always regret what happened with Milla, but he wouldn't sully the gift of life by wasting it on guilt.

He looked at the woman in a hospital bed sleeping in his arms and realised he had a future and that it was just beginning.

Epilogue

Lacey smiled as she looked in the mirror and smoothed the pale blue lace of her dress down. Today she'd stand up and promise God that she'd guide Deacon in life and protect him. She and Gunner were both shocked when Roz and K had asked them to be godparents, but Roz was adamant that her son wouldn't be there without her.

Lacey wasn't sure that was true. Roz would have found a way, she was that type of woman, but it was still an honour. Gunner walked in, looking handsome and sinful in a navy suit with a white shirt and blue tie. Her body reacted instantly, her pulse rate rose, and she felt her nipples tingle with need.

He slipped his arms around her waist and rested his lips against the pulse in her neck. Lacey leaned into him, tilting her head so that he had easier access to her neck. "Hmm."

Gunner raised his head, and his slumberous sexy gaze caught her own in the mirror.

"Keep making noises like that, and we won't make it to the christening."

"How can I help it if you are sexy as sin and that suit makes me want to rip it from your body?"

His eyebrows rose, and a smirk crossed his face. "I think wearing a suit every day could work for me."

Lacey laughed and turned in his arms, looping her arms around his neck. "You'd be crazy in a week, and you know it."

"True. Maybe just weekends then?"

"You're nuts, you know that?"

"Nuts over you, yes."

Lacey felt the place in her heart she thought was already full with her love for this man expand even more. Her feelings for him seemed to grow daily, and she wondered if one day she'd be so full of love, her heart wouldn't be able to take more. She'd shared her thoughts with Skye, who told her love didn't work like that—it was infinite and endless.

"I keep thinking I can't love you more, but then I do, and I wonder how I ever lived without you."

"You won't ever have to find out, Lacey, because I'll never leave you. I wasn't living until I met you. You opened my eyes to the beauty I could have if only I reached for it, but I was afraid. Only you reaching down into the void that was my heart pulled me back to living."

Lacey felt tears prick her eyes. "Gunner, that's beautiful."

"No, Cosmo, it's the truth." He carried on looking at her his eyes dark with desire as he lowered his head and kissed her until she could hardly breathe, the feel of his hands on her ass making her pussy ache to feel him inside her.

He kissed his way down her neck, the tickle of his beard adding to the eroticism as he grazed her breasts through the lace of the dress and she'd have done anything to rip it off and drag him back to bed.

As Gunner got to his knees and looked up at her, she felt so much love for this big, kind man who'd fought so many demons and won.

"I wasn't going to do this now, but I can't wait another second."

Lacey frowned as he reached in his pocket and then her heart stopped as she saw the tiny red box. Tears pricked her eyes as he opened the box to reveal a huge, square-cut diamond. Gunner gently took her hand in his. "Lacey, from the moment we first met, I knew you were special, but it would take years for us to finally find each other again. When we did, I was a man on the brink of despair. You pulled me back and saved me with your love and acceptance, showing me what life could be like. I love you with all my heart and promise you I'll always be there when you need me. I promise to be by your side no matter what. To make you come multiple times a day, to love you, to fuck you when you need it and cherish you when you don't. Please say you will marry me?"

Lacey fell to her knees, not caring about her dress, only the man in front of her and threw her body at him. He caught her and held her to him as she cried before he pulled her back.

"Give me words, Cosmo."

"Yes, I will marry you."

His smile lit the room of the barn conversion they now called home. The other property now owned by Bebe.

Gunner slid the ring on to her finger and then dipped his head so his lips touched hers, and her breath caught at the scent and feel of him like she knew it always would.

160

"Which will it be, Cosmo?"

Lacey frowned.

"Cherish or fuck, because I'm not leaving this house until we've done one or the other, not after I just made you mine."

Her answer was to take his hands and put them back on her ass and squeeze.

"Fuck, good choice."

Then her man fucked her hard, and she loved it because she knew when they got back home, he'd make love to her as if she was the most precious person in the world, because to him she was.

Sneak Peek: Waggs

Aiden Wagner and Willow Yates

Tipping the bottle back, Waggs drained the beer before placing it on the headstone with the other full one. It had been five years had passed since his brother had been laid in the ground at the Camp Nelson National Cemetery, close to his parents' home in Lexington, Kentucky, and not a single day got easier.

Waggs sank to the cold ground and propped his elbows on his knees as he read the headstone.

Aaron Wagner
9th June 1982–8th November 2015
A loving son and brother.

Waggs hated the epitaph that, not for one-second, captured the essence of his twin brother. All of the things written there were true, but Aaron had been so much more than just a son and brother. He'd been a friend, the best damn friend anyone could ever ask for. His best friend. They'd shared everything from the first moment their hearts had begun to beat—first steps, first words, first fight, first girlfriends.

He and Aaron had done everything together, even joined the army together. Then they'd applied for Special Forces Training together where their natural competitiveness had gotten them through ninety-five weeks of gruelling hard work, but they had both got through it, the bond they shared stronger than ever. Ending up in the 5th Special Forces Group stationed at Fort Campbell, Kentucky, together had been the icing on the cake for the brothers who were so close.

Serving alongside Aaron as a Green Beret had been the biggest honour of Waggs' life. He had become a medic, and Aaron had trained as a sniper. Between them, they'd been invincible, able to read each other's thoughts and actions with the eerie accuracy that only twins could do. He'd often known before Aaron did when his

162

brother was sick or hurt, happy or sad, and the same had been the case for Aaron.

When Aaron met Willow Yates, he'd been so damn happy for him, burying his own attraction to her until he was sure he had it under control, that nobody knew he loved Willow too, and not as the sister she'd one day become after Aaron asked her to marry him and she said yes. Then they'd deployed to the sandbox straight after the engagement, and a routine aid mission had gone to hell.

Waggs grabbed the bottle of whiskey and took a swig, enjoying the burn of liquid as painful memories flooded his mind.

A child no older than eight or nine had run up to Aaron in the village, which wasn't unusual; it happened when they visited the villages, keeping peace among the people of Afghanistan. Yet this had been different. Waggs had an awful gut reaction that something was wrong. Everything around him dimmed until he could see the four men at the corner of the village watching the child.

He'd seen the looks of malice and triumph on their faces and he'd known, but before he had a chance to react, the bomb had exploded. The force had thrown him backwards, to the ground, winding him and knocking him senseless for a second, and then he'd rolled, and his vision had blurred. As the smoke receded and he'd seen Aaron, or what was left of him. Waggs had scrambled to his brother, his brain trying to assess the damage. The medic in him knowing it was too late, but the brother fought the horror of reality.

He'd grabbed Aaron's hand as his brother blinked up at him in shock, the bottom half of his body mostly gone, the fact he was still alive giving Waggs false hope.

"Hang in there, Aaron. We're gonna get you some help."

He tried to see what he could do, but even if he had an operating table in front of him, the damage was too extensive. His bottom half was just torn flesh, blood, and gore the stuff of horror movies, but this wasn't a movie; it was his brother's broken body.

"Aiden." His brother coughed, and his lips were covered in the blood from his lungs, which Aiden knew were full of blood.

"I'm here, Aaron."

"I'm scared."

Waggs fought tears as he held on to his brother's hand so tight, willing him to live despite everything. "Don't be scared, Aaron. I won't leave you."

And he hadn't. He hadn't left when his brother drew his last breath and slipped from the world, leaving him alone for the first time in his existence. He sat by his coffin as they waited for a plane to take them home, and he sat by his side on the aircraft. Waggs never left his twin once until they lowered him into the ground and his casket was covered in mud.

Closing his eyes he relived those days over and over, only allowing himself to do it on the anniversary of his brother's death. If he let it out at any other time, then he knew he'd crawl into the ground and die like Aaron had, like he wished every day he had.

His brother had every reason to live, and yet he couldn't save him. It was something he struggled to live with, but it was the guilt of what he'd done next that ate him up every night. It was the reason he fought to help so many find the peace they sought because he'd never have it again.

The funeral had been horrific, his mother sobbing, his father holding her up both physically and mentally, as Waggs had stood stoic in his dress uniform, knowing that if he let the grief free, it would consume him until he was a mess on the ground.

Willow had sat silently crying, with her parents on either side supporting her, and Waggs had once again wished it had been him who died. He loved Willow, and so had his brother. She'd chosen well with Aaron, not that it had been a choice. Nobody knew how he felt, and he'd make sure it stayed that way, but he would look after her.

Aaron had loved her so much and Aiden would make sure she was okay. The only problem was he'd taken it too far; they both had. He'd left Kentucky for his last tour before he retired from the military, his heart no longer in it and hadn't seen her again until the call that changed everything and it shamed him enough that he'd run thousands of miles away and joined Eidolon.

They were his brothers now, and he loved them and would die for them, but nobody would ever replace his twin because they couldn't.

Standing on legs that were unsteady after drinking most of a bottle of liquor, Waggs poured the rest over the headstone. "Love you, bro. I wish every day it had been me who died." He tried to swallow the sob that lurched up to his throat and failed. "I miss you so much, Aaron. I wish you were here, and you could see the beauty you created. If I could go back, I'd make sure you lived. I let you down and I'm so sorry."

Tears tracked down his face as the silence of the cemetery surrounded him, and he let the grief out. Tomorrow he'd shore it up and go home, back to Hereford where he could breathe a little easier from the guilt and shame, but first, he needed to see her.

Walking the few blocks from the cemetery to Willow's home on the outskirts of Lexington, he tried to remember the sound of his brother's voice and couldn't. It made him panic, so he called up his saved messages and played the last one Aaron had sent him. The sound of his brother's voice almost made his legs give way; the loss was so intense. Physical pain never hurt this bad. This was like living with a dagger through the heart.

He got to the red door with pink and purple flowers in the front yard and stopped. Part of him knew he shouldn't be there, that no good would ever come of it, but that didn't stop him knocking on the door. He held on to the frame as he swayed, the alcohol he'd consumed catching up with him.

The door opened, and there she was the love of both his and his brother's life.

Willow gripped the door frame, and he could see him being there hurt her and yet he couldn't stop. She was looking up at him with her dark chocolate brown eyes. Her long lashes swept across her pink cheeks as she closed her eyes briefly, her arms crossed over her middle as if to protect herself. "What are you doing here, Aiden?"

"Please, Willow, I won't stay long."

Willow sighed and his eyes went to her small breasts, her flat tummy, and down to her long-tanned legs that made his mouth water. She was wearing sleep shorts, a tee and looked so young. Yet the pain she held was there in her eyes.

Stumbling past her, he caught her scent, and it was like coming home. It was so familiar and yet hurt so much. Fresh and floral, it danced around him. She uncrossed her arms, and he could see the points of her nipples through the top she wore, her chestnut hair had waves in it today and fell to her shoulders. She looked pretty, but then she always had, even grief hadn't dulled her light.

Moving past him, she opened the bedroom door and moved back. Waggs stopped, staring at the precious form of his sleeping nephew.

165

AJ was just five years old and had been conceived the night before he and Aaron had redeployed. He walked closer and sank to his knees by the bed, looking at the boy who was the image of his father in every way and, therefore, him too. He stroked the blond hair back from his head and wished his brother were there to see his son, to play catch and teach him to ride a bike.

Aaron would be horrified with the way Aiden had abandoned Willow and AJ, but he'd be furious if he knew the rest.

Waggs straightened and saw Willow leaning against the doorjamb, arms crossed over her middle as if it physically pained her to watch him with AJ. He leaned down and kissed the child's head, wishing he were a better man.

Moving back into the hallway of the single-story home, he looked around and saw that it really was a home. Willow had made this a place for her and her son, with pictures of his father around the room, some including him in them, too. He picked one up and studied it, and it showed him and Aaron with their arms around each other's shoulders the day they'd passed their Special Forces training. The smiles on their faces and the hope and excitement were gone now for both of them.

"You can't keep doing this, Aiden. You're only hurting us both."

He turned and looked at her, the peachy flesh of her lips, the curve of her breast in the cheap white t-shirt, and he thought she'd never looked more beautiful.

"I know."

Then he dropped the picture on the side and took her in his arms, backing her against the wall and kissing her like she was the air he needed to breathe. Each tearing at the other clothes as passion and grief, love and betrayal consumed them, and they did the one thing they shouldn't do. It had begun the night they'd buried Aaron, and every year on the anniversary of his death they'd found solace in each other's arms.

It was never spoken of or talked about—it just was. It was the one night he allowed himself to pretend that she was his, that life hadn't dealt them the cruellest of blows. They spent the night in each other's arms and then in the morning he was gone.

She was back to being a mother, and he went back to his life on the other side of the world.

Click here to buy Waggs

Books by Maddie Wade

Fortis Security

Healing Danger(Dane and Lauren)

Stolen Dreams(Nate and Skye)

Love Divided(Jace and Lucy)

Secret Redemption(Zack and Ava)

Broken Butterfly(Zin and Celeste)

Arctic Fire(Kanan and Roz)

Phoenix Rising(Daniel and Megan)

Nate & Skye Wedding Novella

Digital Desire (Will and Aubrey)

Paradise Ties: A Fortis Wedding Novella (Jace and Lucy & Dane and Lauren)

Wounded Hearts (Drew and Mara)

Scarred Sunrise (Smithy and Lizzie)

Zin and Celeste: A Fortis Family Christmas

Fortis Boxset 1 (Books 1-3)

Fortis Boxset 2 (Books 4-7.5

* * *

Eidolon

Alex

Blake

Reid

Liam

Mitch

Gunner

Waggs

* * *

Alliance Agency Series (co-written with India Kells)

Deadly Alliance

Knight Watch

Hidden Obsession

Lethal Justice

Innocent Target

* * *

Ryoshi Delta (part of Susan Stoker's Police and Fire: Operation Alpha World)

Condor's Vow

Sandstorm's Promise (coming soon)

* * *

Tightrope Duet

Tightrope One
Tightrope Two

* * *

Angels of the Triad

01 Sariel

* * *

Other Worlds

Keeping Her Secrets *Suspenseful Seduction World* (Samantha A. Cole's World)

Finding English P*olice and Fire: Operation Alpha* (Susan Stoker's world)

About the Author

Contact Me

If stalking an author is your thing and I sure hope it is then here are the links to my social media pages.
If you prefer your stalking to be more intimate, then my group Maddie's Minxes will welcome you with open arms.

General Email: info.maddiewade@gmail.com
Email: maddie@maddiewadeauthor.co.uk
Website: http://www.maddiewadeauthor.co.uk
Facebook page: https://www.facebook.com/maddieuk/
Facebook group:
https://www.facebook.com/groups/546325035557882/
Amazon Author page: amazon.com/author/maddiewade
Goodreads:https://www.goodreads.com/author/show/14854265.Maddie_Wade
Bookbub: https://partners.bookbub.com/authors/3711690/edit
Twitter: @mwadeauthor
Pinterest: @maddie_wade
Instagram: Maddie Author

Printed in Great Britain
by Amazon

18459932R00102